VALENTINE'S DAY IN VENICE

THE HOLIDAY ADVENTURE CLUB BOOK ONE

STEPHANIE TAYLOR

THE HOLIDAY ADVENTURE CLUB SERIES

BOOK ONE

Valentine's Day in Venice

1

AUGUST 23

AMELIA ISLAND, FL

"Holiday Adventure Club, this is Lucy, how can I help you?" Lucy Landish held the phone to her ear, wedged between cheek and shoulder as she continued tapping away on her computer keys.

She didn't like customers to know that she was still operating a one-woman show at the Holiday Adventure Club office, so she always tried to juggle her various duties and to answer the phone when it rang, even if it meant interrupting her train of thought as she fired off an email.

"Sorry...I think I have the wrong number. I was looking for the Amelia Island Holiday Club?" the man on the other end of the line said, sounding confused.

Lucy let out a quiet sigh. Amelia Island—a small, quaint strip of land loosely connected to the east coast of Florida by a single bridge that crossed the Amelia River—did a brisk tourist trade, but people inadvertently mixed up her business with the sprawling, similarly named hotel on the beach, and most days she ended up just giving them the correct phone number rather than making them hang up and find it themselves. And, after all, even someone who called her by accident could be a potential customer—whether they knew it or not—so Lucy was always helpful because she couldn't afford *not* to be.

"Thank you so much," the man said after Lucy had given him the hotel's phone number.

Lucy set the phone receiver back in its cradle. Starting her own business on a tropical island had been a strategic move, and she still reminded herself daily that this was the direction she'd chosen to go —and for very good reason.

The ringing phone had derailed her train of thought as she'd typed, so Lucy stood up from her desk and stretched her arms toward the low ceiling of the tiny office that was nestled between a coffee shop and a postal store in the strip mall near A1A. She'd been lucky to find a spot so close to the beach, and on nice days when the humidity didn't feel like a pile of bricks on her chest, she loved to prop open the glass front door and breathe in the salty ocean air that blew in off the Atlantic. For most of her life, upstate New York had been home, and with each change of season (though visitors might argue that Florida's only seasons are hot, hotter, and hottest), Lucy appreciated the beach, the humidity, and the fluctuation in the number of tourists. She also appreciated the lack of snow, the way she'd been able to reinvent herself with each mile south that she'd driven from Buffalo, and the fact that her new job didn't have a damn thing to do with death certificates or formaldehyde.

It might seem strange: a thirty-eight-year-old woman leaving a job where her main objective was to identify the cause and manner of death under a variety of mundane and horrifying situations, only to start over as a small business owner whose only job was to be cheerful and to plan people's travel adventures, but it had been the change that Lucy needed in her life in order to keep getting up in the morning. If she'd seen one more mangled body, heard one more tale of unnecessary destruction of a life from a jaded detective, or held one more drug-addled brain, heart, or liver in her gloved hands, she was going to climb into her bed and never crawl out.

Today, however, as Lucy contemplated the pile of work that needed to be done, the late August heat was more than oppressive: it was downright threatening. Her air-conditioning unit rattled a warning that reminded her how much she relied on it, and the sky beyond her wall of windows hung heavy with a line of gray clouds that looked as if they could fall and crush mountains. Within the hour, a heavy rain would pound the roof of her building and the streets outside, and with it would come a quick, ferocious thunderstorm that might knock out the power anywhere on the island without warning.

Lucy abandoned her computer altogether for the moment to stand at the windows, arms folded as she looked out at the impending storm. The parking lot that fronted the row of shops was only half-full, and right outside her office was a vintage Volkswagen Bug painted a cheerful, optimistic shade of yellow with only a few patches of rust. Lucy had been driving it since she'd arrived on Amelia Island a year and a half earlier and sold her VW Passat, bought a tiny bungalow that needed a ton of elbow grease, and signed a lease on the office in the strip mall. None of these acquisitions were really representative of the successful businesswoman she aspired to be, but they were definitely representative of the free-spirited, hopeful, fun-loving girl she'd been once and hoped to eventually be again.

She was working on it. As with all good things, it would simply take some time.

Without locking her office—after all, how hard-up would a burglar have to be to run through the kind of rainstorm that was about to make landfall in order to snatch a PC or a desk phone from a tiny travel agency office?—Lucy stepped out onto the narrow sidewalk and ducked into The Carrier Pigeon, the P.O. box shop next door.

"So, Hurricane Lucy is already making landfall, huh?" Nick Epperson watched her enter as he leaned on the counter of his shop with both elbows. His thin cotton shirtsleeves were rolled and pushed up to reveal tanned, smooth forearms. Nick let the paperback he'd been reading fall shut and he tossed it aside as his gaze focused on Lucy in her above-the-knee floral summer dress. Her auburn hair was wavy and loose around her flushed cheeks, sticking to the back of her neck where the sweat had immediately sprung from her pores in the humidity. As they looked at one another, the first fat drops of rain began to pelt the pavement outside. "You gonna ride out today's festivities with me?"

Lucy glanced around: Nick's shop was as empty as her office. "No customers?"

Nick turned both palms to the ceiling. "I'm becoming obsolete," he said with a charming half-smile. Nick's brown hair was short and mussed, his goatee neatly trimmed. He looked not so much like the proprietor of a business as a grad student who might suddenly pull a dog-eared paperback copy of *The Great Gatsby* from the back pocket of his 501s and start pontificating about how optimism is a noble, if futile, trait.

In truth, he was a mystery writer who lived with a black lab named Hemingway, but his youthful good looks continued to fool bartenders and confound the young women who glanced his way without realizing that he easily had twenty years on them.

"You'll never be obsolete, Epperson," Lucy said, walking over and hopping up on the counter in one easy, fluid movement. She sat with her back to the wall of padded envelopes and shipping boxes as she and Nick faced the rain, watching it hit the windshields of the cars outside with force.

"That's sweet of you to say, but you, my dear, run a travel agency. Now that people can do everything online, neither one of us is really considered 'essential.'"

"Fair enough," Lucy conceded, kicking her legs so that the heels of her sandals banged against Nick's front counter as she sat on it. "But if the fax machine ever makes a comeback, I predict good things for you."

Nick gave an amused chuckle. "And if any generation after the Boomers suddenly gets confused about how to use Travelocity, then I predict great things for *you*. By the way, how is your big project coming along?"

Lucy shrugged her bare shoulders. "I'm wondering if I might be crazy. Or if this is *too* adventurous for the Holiday Adventure Club."

"Going around the world in a year? Seems doable." Nick reached for the paperback he'd cast aside and slid it closer, spinning it on the counter in lazy circles as he talked.

"Yeah, it does, doesn't it?" Lucy watched as a woman holding an umbrella that would be rendered totally useless within seconds exited the nail shop at the end of the strip mall with a fresh manicure. Within seconds, the onslaught of rain drenched the woman and nearly crushed the metal spokes of the umbrella as it began to fold on top of her head. "Yikes," Lucy said as an aside, nodding at the woman. "She better get into her car ASAP and quit running around in a lightning storm holding that thing in the air."

"She does appear to be asking for trouble," Nick agreed, only half watching the woman. "But listen," Nick said, not letting go of his train of thought. "You can definitely hit a city for every major holiday for a year—you're smart and capable and I have the utmost faith in your abilities—but do you *need* to do this?"

Lucy squinted at the rain outside as she thought about it. "I'm *sometimes* smart and *occasionally* capable," she finally said. "And I do need to do this. It's sort of like an internal re-set, you know? It's all part of the process."

Nick, still leaning on the counter next to her, turned his head and looked at her profile for a moment. "He really hurt you, didn't he?" he asked quietly.

In an instant, Lucy's eyes glassed over with unshed tears and her jaw set firmly. She gave a one-shouldered shrug. "He might have left a few contusions. Broken a bone or two. Calcified my heart," she said with a sad smirk. "But I'll survive."

Nick reached over with one lightly clenched fist and gave Lucy a faux punch on the arm. "Look at you. Using your forensic talk to make light of things."

In truth, the man in question had done more than leave a few scrapes; her seven-year marriage had ended—badly—and left her to question everything about her life.

A small, wicked smile tugged at Lucy's lips as a thought formulated. "Hey, since I've got you here, oozing sympathy in my direction, do you think maybe—"

"Nope," Nick interrupted her, pushing away from the counter and holding up his hands in surrender. "I'm not taking care of your evil cat again while you go on vacation. Uh uh. No way."

"Nick," Lucy giggled, watching his face as he backed away, shaking his head. "Joji is the sweetest cat that ever lived! He probably wouldn't even kill a mouse if it was eating my last piece of cheese."

"No, no, and no. I hate cats. They're creepy. And unpredictable. Remember how you told me about that case you had where the woman died and her own cat ate her eyeballs and her lips before the neighbors found her body?" He shuddered. "I will not go near that furry little agent of Satan, no matter how sorry I feel for you. And Hemingway hates cats too."

Lucy slid off the counter as she laughed out loud. "You're too much," she said. "You write books about murder and mayhem, but a ten-pound tabby unravels you." She walked over to the door and rested her fingers on the handle as she looked back at him across the shop. He'd re-settled onto the counter with both elbows and was looking at her with that same easy half-smile he'd had when she walked into the shop. It had been no big secret between them in the year and a half that they'd been friends and neighbors that they found one another attractive, but because of Lucy's relatively recent heartbreak, things had never moved past friendship and mild flirtation.

"Hey, I'm a complicated man," Nick said, lifting his eyebrows and his shoulders slightly. "Are you really going out in that rain?"

Lucy looked back at the downpour. "I'll stay undercover. I just want to run over and get an afternoon coffee."

Nick dropped his eyes to the counter and reached for his book again. "Gotcha," he said flatly. "Stay dry, Lucy."

Lucy pushed open the door and let in the loud rush of pelting rain. The sound of water hitting the roof, the pavement, and the cars in the lot drowned out the last of Nick's words.

SANTO & JOHNNY'S "SLEEPWALK" WAS PLAYING FROM AN OLD-FASHIONED jukebox in the corner of the coffee shop when Lucy walked in thirty seconds after leaving Nick's store.

"Afternoon, Miss Adventure," Dev said, wiping his counter with a wet rag as he glanced up at her. His hazel, almond-shaped eyes were framed by dark lashes that nearly stopped Lucy in her tracks.

Instead, she paused for just a moment as she always did when she first walked into Beans & Sand, caught off-guard once again by Dev's exotic good looks. Dev Lopez was the product of a mother from Jamaica and a father from Mexico, and the combination of the two had yielded light eyes that mesmerized like a kaleidoscope; deeply bronzed skin; soft, curly hair; and broad shoulders. Dev was equally as handsome as Nick, but where Nick was funny and nimble with his words, Dev was serious and pointed. His only concession to joking sarcasm that Lucy had picked up on so far was his penchant for calling her "Miss Adventure," a play on the word "misadventure" and on the name of her business next door. And she loved it, naturally, because in Lucy's experience a good nickname meant you mattered to someone—at least a little.

"Gorgeous afternoon, isn't it?" Lucy shook her left arm, which had been subjected to the sideways-pouring deluge of rain as she'd scurried along the walkway outside, huddling as close to the building as possible. Droplets of water flew all over the floor.

"Get you a coffee to go?" Dev tossed the rag he'd been holding into the stainless steel sink behind the counter and turned to his wide array of coffee supplies and machines. "An afternoon latte? An Americano with coconut milk?"

"Yeah," Lucy said, pulling her hair from the back of her sweat-dampened neck as the song on the jukebox ended and another began. "Actually, I'll have a vanilla latte, please."

Rather than sit, she stood there in the middle of the coffee shop, which had the distinct vibe of a 50s diner with its vinyl covered barstools at the counter, and booths that ran the length of the window. But instead of anything retro and 50s related, Dev had covered the walls with framed posters of his favorite musicians of all eras, including David Bowie, Nirvana, The Smiths, The Beatles, and The Beach Boys. The music ephemera and the colorful jukebox in the corner made it feel like some sort of Hard Rock Cafe outpost.

"Doing good business this week?" Dev asked amiably with his back to Lucy as he made her coffee. Instead of Nick's affable college guy plaid shirt, Dev wore a beat-up black Lenny Kravitz concert t-shirt tucked into well-cut black jeans. He also wore a brown leather belt and brown boots, and on his fingers he wore no fewer than two rings per hand. One wrist was covered in a tangle of leather and string bracelets. Lucy watched as he moved around, admiring his smooth skin. When Dev turned to her with her paper cup of coffee in hand, his serious eyes burned into hers.

She blinked a few times and accepted the coffee with a gracious nod. "I mean...the phone has rung. Does that count?" She smiled at him as she put the cup to her lips for a first sip.

"Careful—that's hot." Dev leaned back against his sink, crossing his boots at the ankles and folding his arms across his strong chest as he watched her intently. "And the phone ringing is a start. Unless it's a wrong number."

"Oof. I feel so exposed," Lucy joked, hoping it would bring a smile to Dev's face. It didn't. Instead his brow furrowed.

"Maybe you should think about your advertising game," he said, looking out the window and staring into the gray sky. "Like, if you've identified who your target travelers are, then you've gotta go to where they are."

"Sage advice," Lucy said wryly, holding the coffee cup with both hands. "I've tried that. Facebook ads, Twitter, retirement community newsletters, college campuses—"

"So basically your audience is everyone?" Dev asked, still watching her closely.

"Yeah, I guess so. Anyone who wants to travel, *can* travel, and who can afford it."

If possible, Dev's brow knitted together even more. "But you're starting with Valentine's Day, right? In Venice, wasn't it?"

Lucy chewed on her bottom lip. "Yeah, and I thought having six months to plan it was a decent head start."

"So, okay. How about gearing this first trip towards romance? Valentine's Day is kind of the ultimate fake romantic holiday, right? And although I've never been there myself, I've heard that Venice is pretty dazzling."

Lucy nodded and picked a spot on the wall on which to focus her gaze. How humiliating to realize that she was already knee-deep into planning this big, groundbreaking business venture, only to have someone point out that she was casting her net too widely. Or at least to remind her that maybe she wasn't cut out to be handling the entire shebang, from soup to nuts. Would it kill her to bring in someone else's ideas or to at least use a friend as a sounding board? Maybe talk to someone who'd spent the last decade working amongst the living and not the dead? Probably not. But in her previous career—and while a forensic pathologist certainly cooperated and worked in conjunction with police, doctors, hospitals, families, witnesses, and sometimes even the FBI—much of her work had been solitary. She'd focused on the task at hand and put all of her mental energy to unlocking the mysteries presented to her by a human who could no longer speak for himself or herself.

"Okay, hit me with what you've got," Lucy said, sipping the hot coffee with a wince.

"I'm just thinking out loud here," Dev said, holding up his hands much as Nick had just done to indicate mock surrender. "But how about advertising on dating sites, dating apps, at matchmaking services—wait, do those still exist? Like actual offices where people go to be matched with eligible suitors?"

"I think so," Lucy said, tucking her hair behind one ear. "Actually, I have no idea. But I'll check it out."

"Oh, and how about seeing if you can leave some brochures with couples counselors or marriage therapists?"

Lucy gave an audible huff. "Wow," she said. "Thank you. I've been so focused on trying to organize the actual trips and to make sure I know where I'm going and what I'm doing that I guess I didn't focus enough on how to get the word out to the right people."

Dev walked over to the jukebox and punched a few buttons. Neil Young's "Harvest Moon" started to play. "Hey, it's not easy manning the ship on your own," he said, running a hand over his close-cropped curls. "I can relate. And I'm full of ideas, so just pop over. Coffee's on the house today," he added, nodding at the cup in her hands.

Lucy laughed. "Good, because I left my wallet in my desk drawer."

"That's okay. I know where to find you if you run out on your tab anyway." Dev blinked his hazel eyes. "Now get over there to your office and write down all my brilliant ideas before we both forget them."

"You got it. And thanks, Dev."

Lucy wasn't entirely sure, but it looked a little—just a tiny bit—like he'd winked at her.

2

DECEMBER 6

PORTLAND, OR

Breanne Wineland-Jones stood at her kitchen sink with a bunch of cilantro in one hand as she watched a family of ducks waddle toward her tiny koi pond in the near-darkness of the December evening.

"What was that?" she asked into the speaker of her iPhone, which was propped up on the counter so that she could FaceTime with her best friend as they made their respective dinners and carried on a conversation simultaneously.

"I said, my friend Erica was at this dating service—you know the one they always advertise on Hulu?—and she saw a flyer about a Valentine's Day trip to Venice. I think it might have been some sort of matchmaking trip or something. Or just a group excursion. Actually, I'm not sure, but it sounded interesting."

Bree shook out the wet cilantro and laid the bunch on top of a paper towel to soak up some of the water. "Mmmhmm," she said, drying her hands. "And are you thinking of going? Or is Erica?"

Carmen Neroli made a disbelieving noise as she banged a pot down on the stove on her end of the line. "No! Erica doesn't fly. She's got some weird fear or something."

"Being afraid to fly is not that weird, Carm. It's a fairly common one," Bree said, reaching for a sharp knife in her butcher block. It never ceased to amaze her how Carmen danced and shimmied through life, shaking off the negative and only hanging onto the things that would bring her joy. More than once Bree had looked at herself in the mirror and pleaded with the universe to make her more like Carmen and less like the always-play-it-safe girl that she actually was.

"I'm more afraid of dying alone than dying on an airplane," Carmen said. "Anyway, I was thinking you and I could go. You know, see if there are any guys out there for us. Okay...wow. Sorry. I don't know if that was the wrong thing to say." Carmen visibly cringed as she waited for her best friend's response.

Bree stopped moving and set the knife on the cutting board. She stared at the plump, ripe tomato she was about to cut into. It had been a year and a half since she'd lost her husband, Kenny, and people were beginning to hint at her dating again, though Carmen had always carefully avoided the topic.

Bree decided to bypass the comment and focus on the trip instead. "Us? Go to Venice?" Her mind immediately conjured images of gondolas and pasta and red wine. It might not be her first choice of a destination to escape to after losing her husband, but it sounded better than Portland in February, which was sure to be gray and rainy and dreary.

"Yeah, girl," Carmen said. "You and me. Hasta la vista, baby. Let's hit the road and see what the world has to offer us."

Bree wandered over to the fridge and stared at the photos she'd taped there: there was one of her as a young, tanned, and carefree twenty-something in Hawaii; another of her accepting her college diploma; and a favorite of hers that showed her holding her infant niece on a porch swing as she sat next to her late husband, Kenny. These were supposed to be her inspiration to remind her of the person she wanted to be: someone who vacationed in the sun; the kind of woman who reached for and achieved her goals; and possibly, someday, a mother.

"So we'd fly to Venice for Valentine's Day?" Bree opened the fridge and took out a block of cheese. Her motivation to prepare and cook a hot meal had vanished as Carmen spoke, and, as she did most evenings, she quickly gave up on cooking and decided to just have some cheese and crackers and a glass of wine.

"I don't know the exact details yet. Erica texted me a picture of the flyer and I'm about to Google this vacation company."

Bree poured her wine and reached for the iPad she kept plugged in on the kitchen counter. "What's it called? The company?"

"Let's see…" Carmen turned off a kitchen timer that was beeping on her end. "It's called Holiday Adventure Club and it's located some-place in Florida. Amelia Island," she said definitively.

"Googling."

"Girl, I thought you were cooking!" Carmen laughed as she leaned toward her own phone screen and frowned at Bree. "Did I just watch you throw in the towel on tacos and take out the cheese and wine again?"

"Indeed you did." Bree scrolled through the homepage for The Holiday Adventure Club as she cut off a hunk of Gruyère with her knife. "Okay, so it looks like the company is actually setting up a year of adventure travel. Each major holiday will take you to a different city, but you can pick and choose or commit to all of them…yadda yadda yadda…and yes, the first one is definitely Valentine's Day in Venice."

"I don't know about you Bree, but I'm down. One hundred percent. Think of all those fiiinnneee looking Italian men. Hot guys in tight pants steering gondolas through the canals. Sexy accents as they take our orders at restaurants…mm mm mm. I am ready to book my ticket *now*."

Bree couldn't help but smile at her friend's enthusiasm. Carmen was someone who'd never met a man she didn't like well enough to spend at least one night with, but never one she'd liked well enough to spend more than a few months with. God love her, but she and Bree were polar opposites when it came to men and dating.

Bree was quiet for a moment before she spoke. "I still have Kenny's life insurance settlement. So it's not the money," she said softly, chewing on the cheese as she looked out the window again to see whether the ducks had gone for a nighttime swim in her miniature pond. "It's just that I was really envisioning myself on some sort of spiritual journey or something. Or maybe soaking up the sun in a tropical location while I forgot about all the months where I cried more than I ate or slept."

"Do you think you'll ever date again?" Carmen asked gently. "I mean, you will, right?"

Unbidden, tears sprang to Bree's eyes and she shrugged. "I don't know," she admitted. "I hope so. I want to." Bree paused. "But I've got to make my wish first." She opened the small drawer that held her pens, scissors, postage stamps, and other loose ends, and she eyed the shiny penny laying inside of a little ceramic dish. For the past year, she'd opened the drawer regularly, looked at the penny, then topped off her glass of wine before tucking in for another evening of Netflix and popcorn.

Carmen gave her a moment before saying softly: "Then let's get out there and get the ball rolling. Because you know what, girl?"

"What?" Bree sniffled.

"Carnival also happens around Valentine's Day, and I wanna run around that gorgeous city in a sparkly mask, slapping the butts of strange men and day-drinking like a madwoman."

Again, Bree laughed, but this time she swiped at a stray tear that had fallen from her eye. "That's it? You want to run around in costume so you can slap men's butts?"

"Honey," Carmen said, giving a suggestive chuckle, "that's just the *start*."

3

FEBRUARY 6

AMELIA ISLAND, FL

Lucy slammed the door of her yellow VW Bug and left it parked at the curb near the tiny corner grocery store that was closest to her house. She had a list of things to buy before her flight to Venice in two days, including snacks for the airplane, and she needed to buy enough cat food to keep Joji fat and happy in her absence. She'd arranged for her next door neighbor Lois to feed her orange tabby, and with luck, Joji would forgive her for her many absences when this year of travel was over.

Inside the shop, Lucy picked up a green plastic basket and slipped it over one arm as she browsed the candy aisle. It had been a while since she'd flown anywhere, and given how little she'd enjoyed the whole experience the last time, she figured that a stack of magazines and an assortment of candy might keep her mind off the turbulence and off her inability to escape from the glorified metal tube as it hurtled through space at breakneck speeds. She'd already tossed a *People* magazine and an issue of *The New Yorker* into her basket along with a box of Hot Tamales and a Butterfinger bar when a familiar voice rang out from the aisle next to hers.

"You like grouper? I can cook a mean grouper and chips," said the male voice, "then serve it up with a nice Chardonnay. You'll love it. I promise."

A woman's tinkling laugh carried through the racks that divided Lucy from the unseen couple. She froze like the linoleum floor beneath her feet had suddenly turned to superglue.

"*Charlie*," the woman said, sounding flirtatious. "I'd eat anything you made for me. If you dish it up, I'll put it in my mouth. You know that." She giggled again, this time sounding wicked and suggestive.

Lucy rolled her eyes.

The man—Charlie—gave a light growl and the woman's surprised laugh drowned out the instrumental version of Madonna's "Borderline" that was playing on the overhead speakers. Lucy could only imagine that he was pulling her close and nuzzling her neck with his whiskery cheeks. She looked up and down the aisle, wondering what the best move would be: drop the basket right there and make a break for it? Find someone to hide behind all the way to the register and hope that Charlie wouldn't actually see her? But which direction should she go? She felt panic rising in her chest, and instead of setting the basket on the floor and forgetting about it altogether, she rushed down the aisle in the direction of the front door, basketful of candy and magazines bumping against her hip as she dodged a gray-haired woman whose motorized scooter was on a direct collision course with an end-cap made up of at least a hundred of boxes of saltines. Normally Lucy might have stopped to help redirect the woman, but instead she stepped around her and kept moving.

Unfortunately, the couple in the next aisle had decided to go the same direction, and without warning, Lucy found herself face-to-face with her ex-boyfriend and the giggly vixen on his arm.

"Lucy! Hey!" Charlie's tone was jovial but forced, though he did sound truly surprised to see her. Given the size of the island they lived on and the inevitability of them running into one another at some point, it didn't seem all that surprising to Lucy, just unfortunate.

Lucy stopped short just as she reached the front door with the basket still in her hands.

"Hi, Charlie," she said, drawing herself up to her full height and trying her best to look dignified. Standing next to Charlie with her pink-painted mouth agape was Katrina, Lucy's former roommate. The open mouth could have been read as shock by someone less acquainted with Katrina, but Lucy knew her well enough to know that this was simply her face. Her annoying, mouth-breathing, dumb-as-rocks face. They'd only lived together for the first six months of Lucy's time on Amelia Island as she'd searched for a more permanent living solution, but it had been plenty long enough.

"Whatcha got there?" Charlie peered into her basket with amusement as Katrina instinctively drew closer to him, looping her arm through his and angling her body coquettishly so that her pushed-up breasts were grazing his upper arm. She tossed her fluffy blonde hair over one shoulder and then ran a hand covered with long, pink lacquered nails through the ends of it. "Looks like the makings of a solid Friday night."

"It's for my trip," Lucy said. "On the airplane. I don't like to fly. Remember?" The encounter was going awkwardly so far, and Lucy was reminded of a time when she'd caught herself alone in the room where autopsies were done at the Erie County Medical Examiner's office in Buffalo, talking to a friendly-looking corpse about her plans for the weekend when a coworker had walked in. *That* had actually been less awkward than this exchange.

Charlie gave an uncomfortable laugh, as if the three of them were somehow supposed to ignore the fact that he'd been dating Lucy when she'd come home and caught him in a compromising position with Katrina, and that he knew all kinds of details about Lucy and her life.

"Yeah, I remember," Charlie finally said. He at least had the decency to put one hand in the pocket of his mint green shorts and to look away. "So where are you off to?"

Lucy paused for a moment, then took his gaze head-on. "Venice."

"Venice? As in Italy?" Both of Charlie's eyebrows lurched upwards and he pulled his chin back, clearly waiting for the punchline of the joke. "A girl who hates to fly jetting off to Europe?"

"Yep, she is," Lucy said, trying to keep her voice even. She refused to let Charlie and Katrina see her falter. "The Holiday Adventure Club is launching a yearlong round-the-world journey. On each holiday we'll be somewhere different. Like, Valentine's Day is in Venice, St. Patrick's Day will be in St. Barts—"

"And Thanksgiving will be in Turkey?" Charlie interjected, laughing at his own lame attempt at humor.

It was just like him to interrupt someone with a tragically unfunny quip and then derail everything by laughing too hard and too long. Even though she'd been reasonably attracted to Charlie when they'd met during her first few weeks on the island, he'd always reminded her of a finance bro who was mediocre at golf, got drunk off of two beers, and whose humor was both dull and blisteringly offensive at the same time. Maybe she'd just been lonely and vulnerable after leaving her whole life behind in New York, because seeing him here with Katrina didn't elicit even an ounce of jealousy. Of course they hadn't been together long enough for him to hurt her. And maybe she'd already been hurt so badly that her heart barely registered Charlie's highly predictable and unoriginal betrayal.

"Probably not," Lucy said with a weak smile. It suddenly struck her as bizarre that she hadn't bumped into him in over a year, but now that she had, it felt oddly like gaining closure on the whole situation. She wrinkled her nose in distaste as Charlie set a hand on Katrina's ass, and suddenly even the memory of him looking over his shoulder at her as Katrina peered at her guiltily from under his arm as they coupled on her couch—*her couch*—seemed like nothing but a distant memory. Like a bad movie she'd once seen.

"I think it sounds cool, Lucy," Katrina offered, though she didn't make direct eye contact and she didn't let go of Charlie's arm. In fact, she arched her back a bit more, leaning into Charlie like a wildcat desperate to mark its territory. If only Lucy had the guts to tell her that she could chill out—no one in the grocery store was interested in stealing her dumb ape of a boyfriend—but instead she just gave Katrina a quick, close-lipped smile that undoubtedly looked as insincere as it felt.

"I hope it goes well," Charlie said, raising a hand as if he were making an imaginary toast to her.

"Thanks. Anyway. I have some things I need to get for the trip, so...it was...well, maybe we'll run into each other again sometime." Lucy gave a curt nod.

"On Amelia Island?" Charlie shot her a crooked half-smile. "Chances are good we'll see each other again."

The minute they were gone, Lucy exhaled. She felt proud of herself: she'd survived her first run-in with her ex and her ex-roommate, and she'd somehow stopped short of fleeing the store with stolen magazines and candy. Rather than set her items down and leave the shop, she squared her shoulders and went right back to the candy aisle, where she promptly added M&Ms, two bags of jelly-beans, and a box of Milk Duds to her basket.

She'd survived Charlie and Katrina (both names of fairly memorable hurricanes, she noted to herself), and now there was no question—she'd get through this flight and put even more miles between herself, her old life, and every failed relationship and disappointment she'd ever had.

4

FEBRUARY 7

AMELIA ISLAND, FL

L ucy spent the morning at Honey's, the tiny salon at the end of the strip mall that did manis and pedis dirt cheap. The owner, Honey Joplin, was an Amelia Island native and a bonafide character. Well into her sixties, Honey knew no bounds when it came to flirting with men, and she was well-known around the island for sharing her opinions based on messages that she claimed to receive from the universe.

"Hiya, Papaya!" Honey called out, as she did every single time Lucy slipped through the front door and angled herself around the oversized ceramic flower pots and miniature running fountains that filled the small shop.

"Hi, Honey. Do you have time for a pedi before I hit the road?" Lucy ducked under the plethora of hanging ferns and African violets that had nearly overrun the racks of nail polish.

In response, Honey slid across the floor on her wheeled stool and twisted the knob of the foot bath to fill it with water. "For you? I got time." She patted the chair that was perched above the foot bath and motioned for Lucy to sit. "And I want to hear all about your big adventure. Tell me everything: how many hot guys will be there, all the places you'll be going, and what your limit is for men you'll kiss on one trip. Details. Now. Go." Honey looked at her over the top of her bifocals.

A woman who had been waiting near the front door for her manicure to dry called out a good-bye to Honey, who waved in response.

"I'm headed to Venice, and I'm pretty nervous," Lucy admitted, kicking off her flip-flops and using the small step next to the pedicure chair to climb up onto the leather seat. She dipped her foot into the water gingerly, making sure it wasn't too hot for her. "Aaahhh," she said, letting her feet drift to the bottom of the basin as the water worked its way up her calves.

"Nervous? Don't you entertain even *one* negative thought about this trip, do you hear me?" Honey turned off the water and pushed her reading glasses up into thick, curly brown hair that was shot through with silver streaks. She looked up at Lucy from her lower position and narrowed her eyes. "I've actually been meaning to pop down to your office this week and let you know the messages I've been getting."

"Oh?" Lucy tried not to let her eyebrows shoot into her hairline at the mention of Honey's "messages," as she was still undecided about her stance on psychic powers and words of wisdom from The Great Beyond—both specialties of Honey's and both very popular topics among her regular customers.

Honey reached for a new, sterile packet of pedicure tools. She tore the plastic open and dumped the tools onto her little work bench. "I've been hearing all week from my spirit guides that your mission for this trip to Italy is to reunite a stranger with something important that they've lost."

Lucy frowned. "That's a little vague. Anything more detailed?"

Honey looked into the swirling water as she poured a packet of lavender scented skin softener into the basin and swirled it around with her hand. "Not really. Just someone you don't know yet who needs to find something they've lost. That's all I've got." She turned off the water and looked up at Lucy. "What color do you want on your toes this time?"

Lucy puckered her lips. "How about something for Valentine's Day? Red, maybe?"

Honey closed her eyes and shook her head. She looked deeply disappointed by Lucy's lack of imagination. "Too basic. How about pastel pink with little red hearts?"

"I am putty in your hands, Honey. Just make me gorgeous." Lucy laced her fingers together in her lap and leaned her head back as Honey pulled one foot from the water and rested it on the edge of the basin so that she could buff it with a pumice stone.

"Too late," Honey said, looking up at her much younger friend with a wink. "You're already gorgeous. Just ask your two next door neighbors."

Lucy's head lifted from the back of the chair as she snapped to attention. "What are you talking about, Honey?"

Honey stopped what she was doing and looked at Lucy incredulously. "Are you kidding me?" She waved the pumice stone that was attached to a plastic handle in the direction of the front door. "You think I don't see you running over to Nick's shop three times a day? Does anyone have that much mail to send?"

Lucy's cheeks flamed.

"Oh? Is that not it?" Honey feigned innocence. "Then maybe you're going over there to see if he has a package to deliver," she said with a lascivious gleam in her sharp blue eyes.

"Honey!" Lucy laughed. "We're just friends. Nick is...a good listener."

"Mmmhmm," Honey agreed, squirting a glob of sugar scrub into her left hand and reaching for Lucy's foot. "And is Dev also a good listener? Or maybe you're willing to risk overdosing on caffeine everyday just to get one more sip of his delicious coffee?"

Lucy couldn't help it—she laughed. "Honey," she said, blinking a few times. "I mean. They're both cute—"

"Damn straight they are," Honey agreed, scrubbing Lucy's foot with vigor. "I might be old enough to be their mother, but I'd diaper and burp either of those boys without a second thought."

"Ew." Lucy's nose wrinkled as she laughed again. "Let's talk about you, Honey. How is Milt?"

Honey's mouth quirked up on one side and she dropped Lucy's foot back into the water unceremoniously and motioned for Lucy to give her the other one. "Milton Burns? That old coot," Honey said, shaking her head as she dumped more foot scrub into her hand. "He left to head up to Georgia and said he'd call when he got back, but do you think that fool picked up his phone and actually dialed my number? No, he sure did *not*. And I even saw him walking out of the store yesterday morning with a six-pack of Budweiser and a bag of hot dog buns. He'd better not call me ever again if he knows what's good for him."

The conversation went on like this for the rest of the pedicure, leaving both women in stitches as they recounted Honey's string of ill-fated Amelia Island love affairs dating all the way back to the Seventies. When Lucy finally left, it was with her wallet thirty dollars lighter, toes that looked like they'd been dipped in pink frosting and sprinkled with red candy hearts, and with one more psychic prediction: that someone would fall into a canal while Lucy was in Venice.

She was back in her office that afternoon and running around printing information for the trip and tying up loose ends when she heard someone clear his throat at the front door. Lucy spun around, hands full of printer paper.

"I see candy. Lots and lots of candy," Nick said, standing in the doorway to The Holiday Adventure Club office with a box wedged under one toned arm, clad in nothing but a fitted white t-shirt and a pair of loose shorts that made him look like a surfer. "Is it Halloween?"

Lucy shook her head. She would have answered him right away, but her mouth was full of M&Ms.

"Well, this is for you," Nick said, holding the box in the air lightly on the tips of his fingers like he was delivering a box of pizza. "Came in this morning."

Lucy finished chewing the candy and swallowed. "No, it's not Halloween. This is supposed to be my airplane stash, but I got nervous and dug into it early," she said, waving at the open grocery store bag on her desk. Nick leaned over and peered inside.

"Wow. That's an impressive amount of sugar."

Lucy shrugged. "It probably won't last till I'm on the plane. Anyway, what's in the box?"

Nick set it on the desk and folded his arms, considering the box as if he might be able to guess its contents. "Dunno. It's generally frowned upon for me to open the packages that arrive at my mail store addressed to others. And it just kind of feels wrong, you know?"

Lucy pulled a sharp letter opener from the cup on her desk and looked at the box. "I wasn't expecting anything."

It was Nick's turn to shrug. "Cute toes," he said, looking at her feet. "So do you think you're ready for Venice?"

"Thanks—I let Honey choose the color. And I'm ready as I'll ever be. I've been planning this trip for six months, so I honestly have no excuse *not* to be ready." Lucy slit the tape that covered the flaps of the box and opened it. She shoved a hand inside and fished around. "And I can't back out now regardless, because when I was at the store buying all this garbage," she said, waving the letter opener in the general direction of the candy, "I ran into Charlie and Katrina."

"Oof."

"*Major* oof. I heard them before I saw them and they caught me making a break for the door with a basketful of Butterfingers and *People* magazines. I looked like I had raging PMS."

Nick blew out a breath. "Okay, so you had your first run-in. Which is amazing that it took this long, but that's cool. Gave you more time to process."

"I needed far more time than that to process seeing my boyfriend's naked behind on top of my no good, backstabbing, tramp-stamped, fired-from-every-job-she-ever-had ex-roommate. And you know what?" Lucy said, building up momentum as she spoke. "I probably should have known she was bad news the minute I caught her clipping her toenails at the kitchen table."

Nick's face contorted with disgust. "Dear God, that is *not* okay."

"You think that's bad? I also once walked into the living room and found her sitting on the couch, laughing as our neighbor who was in a wheelchair tried over and over to wheel herself up the ramp after a rainstorm. She just giggled and watched her roll backwards every time."

"No! Shut up. This did not happen."

"I swear it did. Oh! And then she pulled out her phone and started taking video."

"Lucy. Under no circumstances should it have surprised you that this hideous creature slept with your boyfriend. Seriously. We are not the least bit shocked by the outcome. At least not anymore."

Lucy's head dropped and she closed her eyes for a moment. "I know. Believe me, I know. It was seriously the last straw for me. I came down here to start over, and—well, it's all history now. All of it."

Nick pulled out one of the chairs that sat on the opposite side of Lucy's desk. He perched on the edge, elbows on his knees as he bent forward and watched her remove a smaller box from inside the big box he'd brought over.

Lucy held it up and squinted, inspecting the fine print. "It's a snow globe."

"A snow globe?"

She opened the small box and slid out a round bubble-wrapped item, carefully unwinding the wrapping and tossing it aside. Lucy held up a crystal clear snow globe toward the sunlight streaming in through the front window. Suspended inside was an entire universe of glitter, spinning around a classic Venetian scene: buildings along a canal with a row of gondolas manned by what appeared to be tiny jovial, singing gondoliers.

"Ooooh," Lucy said softly. "It's so pretty." She set it on the edge of her desk, watching as the gold glitter danced in the sun. "But who sent this to me?" She reached into the box and dug out the packing slip, unfolding it and skimming the information. "No name on the sender line."

Nick slapped his knees a little too loudly and stood up. "Well. The mystery continues, I guess."

"Yeah," Lucy said, still looking at the snow globe. "I guess it does."

"Hey." Nick stopped at the open door, standing there as a gentle February breeze blew in off the sea and ruffled his already mussed hair. "I hope you have an amazing trip. And I hope you get a little of *la dolce vita* while you're there."

Lucy watched him for a moment. "Yeah, I hope so too, Nick. I'll see you when I get back."

He lifted a hand and stepped through the doorway to head back to his shop.

It wasn't until after he'd gone that Lucy finally picked up the snow globe again and turned it over. Just as she'd suspected, it had a key and once she'd wound it, the little music box began to play a tune.

It was *La Dolce Vita.*

5

FEBRUARY 11
VENICE, ITALY

Bree and Carmen stood in the middle of their hotel suite in Venice, jet-lagged and stunned that they'd actually done something other than work all day and then call each other from their respective kitchens as they pieced together their dinners and kvetched about coworkers and bosses over wine.

"We're in Venice." Bree blinked a few times, looking at the giant floor-to-ceiling windows that let in a wash of sunlight. The room felt warm despite the fact that it was the middle of February.

"And it's Carnival," Carmen added, turning to look at her friend. "We're in one of the most gorgeous, historic cities in the world, and we have zero responsibilities. Do you know what this means?"

Bree was too tired to guess. "What does it mean?"

With a whoop that nearly made Bree pee her pants in surprise, Carmen tossed her purse in the general direction of a chair by the window and took a running leap onto the king-sized bed. Her joyous shouts grew louder and more insistent as she jumped up and down on the bed, throwing out her arms and kicking her legs wildly with each bounce.

"Carmen..." Bree said, watching her with exhausted awe. Where did her friend even find the energy for stunts like this? Carmen had spent the entire flight flirting with a flight attendant who looked like a male model instead of trying to get some sleep, and when they'd disembarked, she'd raced through the airport looking for snacks and souvenirs like an Energizer Bunny on crack. "That's *my* bed."

"Then get your butt up here, girl!" Carmen shouted, landing on her backside with a bounce.

"If I get onto that bed, the only thing I'm doing is taking a nap," Bree warned.

Carmen fell back on the bed so that her head hit one of the pillows. "You know. I could nap, now that you mention it."

Bree kicked off her boots and climbed onto the mattress, crawling up next to her friend and resting her head on the other pillow. "Ahhh," she said. She closed her eyes and pulled her knees towards her chest as she curled up comfortably on her side with her back to Carmen. "Now *this* is more like it."

"You're right, Bree," Carmen said, placing a hand gently on Bree's back. "Let's get some shut eye, girl. No more monkeys jumping on the bed."

"At least not for now," Bree mumbled, feeling herself fall into a state of relaxation. "Maybe the monkeys can jump later."

"That's right, girl. Maybe later."

AS SHE DOZED, BREE DREAMED FIRST OF HER WEDDING DAY, AND THEN of the last day of Kenny's life. It was the deep, underwater sleep of jet lag and pure exhaustion and it pulled her into a world of vivid images and memories.

Kenny's blue eyes as she'd stepped up to the altar at the church and he'd looked down at her in her wedding gown for the first time. Kenny's blue eyes looking overly large and tired in his thin face in the hospital bed, pleading with her to let him go. Kenny's blue eyes smiling at her from the framed photo of the two of them on vacation in Colorado that she still kept on her nightstand.

The diagnosis had been grim, and ALS had proved a swift and

merciless thief, sweeping into their lives when she and Kenny had both just turned thirty. Within eighteen months, he was gone. It still made Bree reel to think of all she'd lost and of all the time she still had ahead of her without him. Knowing that her husband was being ravaged from the inside out by an unforgiving, unstoppable disease had left Bree unhinged. She'd gone to dark places she hadn't even known existed, and to this day there was no one—not even Carmen —to whom she could completely unburden herself when it came to the thoughts she'd had on the many sleepless nights following Kenny's death.

Kenny was a CPA. He'd been pragmatic and reliable—the one who remembered which month to plant certain flowers or how long it had been since they'd rotated their mattress. He was the kind of guy (the very rare kind, according to Bree's friends) who had bought his own parents' birthday gifts rather than counting on his wife to do it. He'd never forgotten an anniversary. Things with Kenny were always predictable, but in a nice way, Bree thought, feeling a tiny bit defensive of Kenny's reliability.

She, on the other hand, was the dreamer. The one who thought maybe running a vegan baked goods food cart might be the key to her own personal fulfillment (they were living in Portland, after all). It was Bree who wanted to throw caution to the wind and birth control pills into the trash on their wedding day and start dreaming of babies, but Kenny had crunched the numbers, and he was sure that they were at least three years from being able to afford even one, much less the three or four kids that Bree had hoped for.

And now, in Kenny's absence, it was as if she'd absorbed some of his caution in order to keep the universe in balance. Rather than meeting up with friends for Moscow Mules before an opening at the Portland Art Museum, she now stayed in and ordered fried rice and egg rolls and watched Hulu. Instead of trying to convince Kenny to take a Latin dance class at the rec center near their house as she'd done so many times, she now did crosswords and listened to NPR and did the absolute bare minimum at her job as a book buyer for Powell's Bookstore. She wasn't sure how much longer her boss would accept the amount of effort she was currently giving; even young widows had to climb back on the horse at some point and keep riding.

"Hey, girl," Carmen said gently, shaking Bree's shoulder. "You awake?"

Bree sat up abruptly in the early evening half-light. Her shoulder-length dark brown hair was tousled, and a pink line from her pillow ran vertically down one cheek. "No?" It came out as more of a question than an answer as she rubbed her eyes with the heels of both hands.

"You were making funny noises and I got worried." Carmen sat up and reached over to turn on the bedside lamp. "I thought maybe we should get up anyway and go to the little welcome party thing down in the lobby. Even if we don't want to."

"We don't want to," Bree said definitively, shaking her head.

"Ahhh! I knew you'd say that!" Carmen pushed herself up to a standing position and stretched both arms overhead. "And I know you'd like to go back to sleep, but that's a terrible idea. If we do that now, we'll be awake again at three in the morning."

Bree groaned and flopped back onto the bed, flinging an arm over her eyes to block out the light. "Are you sure it's a good idea to go and meet people like this?"

There was no question that she looked like hell after the long flight and the dream-filled nap, and the last thing Bree wanted to do was mingle with a group of women in matching tracksuits who'd come to Venice to celebrate the fact that they were all turning sixty this year. Or a couple there to mark their thirtieth wedding anniversary. Or—god forbid—a bunch of cheesy single guys who'd come on the trip hoping to score.

Carmen walked around the room, turning on as many lights as she could. "I'm absolutely sure we need to go. And I'm also going to find a Diet Coke to wake you up. I'll be right back."

True to her word, Carmen dug a room key from Bree's purse and went out in search of caffeine, leaving Bree alone to wake up slowly. She stood and walked over to the floor-to-ceiling windows that looked out onto the canal below. Bree watched gondoliers steering their passengers across the navy blue water as the sun began its slow dive over a city that she had already realized was magical.

"Here you go, girl," Carmen said, elbowing her way into the room and letting the heavy door slam behind her. She held out a short, squat bottle of cold Diet Coke for Bree. "You should drink up while you, like, fix that face or something." Carmen made a sweeping motion with her hand and threw a pained grimace at Bree to let her know that she was basically a hot mess.

Bree sighed and took the bottle of soda from her. She twisted the lid and took a big, fizzy gulp that made her eyes squint and her lips pucker. "Okay, I'll fix myself as much as I can. But no promises."

THIRTY MINUTES LATER THE TWO WOMEN STOOD IN THE MIDDLE OF THE lobby, Carmen wearing tight black jeans and lots of silver jewelry, Bree in a pink wool wrap dress and brown leather boots. There were about twenty other people gathered in various states of exhausted repose, some draped over couches and overstuffed chairs, others standing awkwardly with no place to put their hands.

"Hello, everyone!" A young woman with reddish-brown hair pulled up in a topknot stepped into the center of the group. The heavy chandelier above the lobby cast sparks of light all over her and she looked around with curiosity, taking in each face as she turned in a circle. "It's so good to see you all in person. I'm Lucy Landish, and I'm thrilled that you all decided to join me on this first Holiday Adventure Club trip!"

"I wonder if she flew first class and slept the whole way?" Carmen hissed, leaning over to Bree and nudging her with an elbow as she scanned Lucy's smooth turtleneck sweater and jeans. "She's too peppy for those of us who are severely sleep deprived. Must be a Florida thing."

Lucy clapped her hands together. "We have exciting things planned for our seven days in Venice, and whether you're here with a loved one, or just along for the ride to see whether romance finds you in The Floating City, I want to officially welcome you to Valentine's Day in Venice!"

There was a smattering of light applause as people glanced around at one another, checking to see who was already paired off or who might be a singleton hanging off the side of the group like a barnacle clinging to a boat.

"Are you two lovebirds?" A man with a thick Jersey accent leaned in close to Bree and Carmen. His eyebrows looked like fuzzy black caterpillars, and there was a sheen of sweat over his top lip. Involuntarily, both women took a step back.

"We are," Carmen said confidently, reaching over and lacing her fingers through Bree's. "This is our honeymoon."

The man's eyes gleamed a little bit brighter and his already heavy breathing cranked up a few notches. Just then, a plump, overly made-up woman strode across the lobby and moved in close to Mr. Eyebrows. She eyed Bree and Carmen warily.

"Well, congratulations, you two," the man said, rubbing his thumb against the pads of his other fingers as he looked them up and down like he was sizing up a couple of prize-winning horses. "I bet you'd make some beautiful babies together."

"Richard!" the woman said, slapping the back of her husband's meaty neck so hard that it sounded like she was trying to kill a mosquito. Her mouth hung open in shock. She looked angry.

"*What*, baby," he said, sounding annoyed. "It's their honeymoon. I'm just wishing them good luck."

Carmen tugged Bree away, but didn't let go of her hand even when they were safely across the lobby.

"Ew. That guy was way too much for me at this particular moment," Bree said as a waiter with a tray of champagne flutes walked in the direction of the group. "Hey, do you think those are for us?"

Lucy started lifting glasses and passing them around to the Holiday Adventure Clubbers. Her face was animated and her eyes bright as she chatted with each person individually.

"What do you think—uppers?" Carmen asked conspiratorially, lifting her chin in Lucy's direction. "Maybe a stiff drink before she came down from her room? Or maybe she's just a tiny bit high?"

Bree tipped her head as she watched Lucy chatting up two women who were obviously identical twins—dressed the same all the way down to their clean, white Keds—and who couldn't have been less than seventy-five years old if they were a day.

"I dunno. She just seems excited. I bet she worked really hard to plan all this, and she wants it to go well."

Carmen sighed. "Wow. Way to call me out for being a big bitch," she said, folding her arms across her ample chest. "You always see the silver lining in everything, you know? I actually kind of admire that." She smiled at her friend. "I'll never be able to emulate it, but I do admire the hell out of it."

With a shrug, Bree reached out for a champagne flute as the waiter walked past them. "I'm not so sure about that, Carm, but you know what I am sure about?" She blinked a few times; her eyes felt puffy and sore. "I'm sure that after this glass of champagne I'm gonna be ready for bed for *real*."

Carmen snatched a flute from the tray with a small nod in the waiter's direction. She lifted her glass and clinked it against Bree's. "Same, girl. Same."

They downed their champagne in unison and then Carmen put an arm around her friend's shoulders to lead her back to the elevators. She made sure to send a long, suggestive wink in the direction of icky New Jersey Richard when his wife wasn't looking.

6

FEBRUARY 12

VENICE, ITALY

I t was three a.m. local time and Bree was wide awake. She pulled on a sweater over her leggings and t-shirt and stumbled down to the nearly empty bar in the hotel lobby, where a motley collection of humans sat quietly with their various beverages of choice, shoulders rounded, eyes tired.

At the counter, Bree rested both elbows on the smooth cherry wood, waiting for the bartender to deliver her vodka with a splash of cranberry juice over ice. If she wasn't going to sleep, she was at least going to feel mellow.

"Breanne, right?" A woman sidled up to her and planted herself on the high-backed bar chair next to Bree's. "I'm Lucy." She thrust a hand in Bree's direction and set her own highball glass on the counter.

"You can call me Bree," Bree said, taking Lucy's hand wearily. "I couldn't sleep." She loved that Lucy was in a gorgeous, sumptuously decorated bar in Venice at three o'clock in the morning wearing a pair of yellow flannel pajamas covered with floating cartoon donuts.

"I've been here for two days, and I haven't slept right yet." Lucy shrugged and crossed her legs under the lip of the bar as if she were decked out in a ballgown and heels instead of her flannels and a pair of hot pink fuzzy slippers.

"Not good with traveling?" Bree asked conversationally.

The bartender had an ink black goatee and bulging, tattooed forearms. He set a drink in front of Bree and she lifted it gratefully.

"It's not that, really," Lucy admitted, dragging her glass through the little pool of condensation that it left on the wood. "I'm just feeling a bit...rootless. I moved to Florida about a year and a half ago, and when I did, I left everything behind. A broken relationship. My career. My mom." She tipped her head to one side. "And now I just feel like everyday I'm waiting to wake up and be at *home*."

"Well, I wake up everyday in my actual home, but it doesn't feel like it anymore," Bree said, taking a long pull on her drink and feeling the alcohol's warmth as it released some of the tension inside of her.

"Maybe that's the human condition." Lucy stared at the way the chandelier lights played off the mirror behind the bar. "Maybe we just spend our time seeking out that place that feels right," she paused, "that feels like it's *ours*."

"Maybe you're right." Bree lifted her glass and waited for Lucy to clink hers against it before they both took another sip.

"Can I ask," Lucy started. She waited a beat before going on. "Are you hoping to find romance on this Valentine's trip? Or is it just you and your friend here for fun? Oh!" Lucy's hand flew up and she covered her mouth. "God, I'm so sorry. Maybe you and your friend are here on a romantic trip together—I didn't mean to assume anything. The Holiday Adventure Club is open to anyone and everyone and I would never—"

Lucy looked so stricken and apologetic that Bree had to laugh and cut her off. "No, no. It's okay! Carmen is my best friend. She's always looking for a few good men," Bree said. "But I'm here because...well, this is my first trip as a widow." She tried the words out and let them sit in the air for a moment before going on. "My husband died of ALS, and Carmen really wanted me to get out of Portland. Pretty much all I've done for the past year is work, come home, sleep, and get up so I could go to work again." Bree held her glass with both hands and stared down at the ice cubes floating in pink liquid. "So. Yeah. That's basically it."

Lucy swallowed hard. "I'm so sorry, Bree. I think you're really brave for coming on this trip."

Bree lifted one shoulder, let it fall. "I'm not sure if taking a trip counts as an act of bravery, but here I am."

"I think it does. For whatever that's worth. Life is hard and sometimes the easy thing to do is retreat, so good for you that you're resisting that. I think it's amazing."

Bree swallowed and pulled her lips back from her teeth, making an *aaahh* sound as she set her glass on the bar. "You know, Lucy. You're right. The fact that we're both out here, searching for something, is a good thing."

The bartender switched on a small speaker behind the bar as he dried glasses and stacked them on a shelf. Nirvana's unplugged version of "The Man Who Sold the World" played quietly while he worked.

Lucy knocked back the rest of her drink and set it on the bar with a nod. "I actually feel like I could sleep now. How about you?"

Bree pushed her empty glass toward the bartender and dug into her purse to find some money. "You know, I think I could sleep." She dropped a few euros on the bar and stood. "See you in the morning?"

Lucy looked at her Apple watch with its lime green wristband and smiled. "I'll see you a little *later* in the morning."

"Goodnight, Lucy," Bree said, walking toward the elevators.

"'Night, Bree."

BREAKFAST THE NEXT MORNING WAS STRONG COFFEE WITH BREAD, rolls, butter, and jam in the hotel's light-filled restaurant on the ground floor. The weather was gorgeous again, and through the windows, the diners could see the hustle and bustle of Carnival tourists and locals going about their daily lives on Venice's ancient cobblestone streets. Bree was still exhausted and more than a little fuzzy from her middle-of-the-night drink, but she stumbled into the dining room and looked around, taking in the bright-eyed members of the Holiday Adventure Club group that she recognized from the night before.

"I'll ask for our own carafe of coffee," Carmen told her, physically turning Bree around and giving her a light shove in the direction of an empty table near the windows of the hotel restaurant. Bree sat down and immediately commenced staring into space, watching the way the winter sun glittered off the canal as she waited for coffee. Two or three gondolas slid by, laden with humans going places as Bree wondered what it would be like to live in a city with no cars.

"Earth to Breanne," Carmen said, placing a white carafe in the center of the table. "You there, girl?" Carmen was already dressed to the nines, with her thick mane of honey brown curls loose around her light brown face, and a pair of oversized gold hoops dangling from her ears. She sat down across from Bree and tapped the French-manicured fingers of one hand against the table as she watched her friend with concern.

"I brought the lucky penny," Bree said as she reached for her coffee. Carmen lifted an eyebrow.

Across the restaurant, Lucy greeted the other guests with the kind of cheer that could only be manufactured this early by copious amounts of caffeine. She was handing out yellow printed sheets of information about their first full day in Venice. "Should I go and get one of those papers?" Bree asked, pointing at Lucy.

"We'll grab one on our way out." Carmen's eyes stayed on Bree. "You brought the penny?"

Bree nodded, pouring a thin stream of heavy cream into her coffee and then stirring it with a spoon. She remembered the day she'd finally emptied out the drawer next to Kenny's side of the bed. Alongside a handful of baseball cards from the 90s was a stack of handwritten notes that he'd saved from his grandma, a map of the New York City subway system from 2011, and the copper penny that he'd worn inside his shiny black shoe on their wedding day for good luck.

It was the penny she kept in a ceramic dish in her kitchen drawer now, and finding it had knocked Bree sideways. During the last days that Kenny could speak intelligibly in the hospital, he'd grabbed her hand and rasped as he fought to get the words out.

"Make a wish, Bree," he'd said, looking into her hazel eyes with his icy blue ones. "Take the penny somewhere amazing and make a wish for me."

She'd promised that she would, but in the fog of loss and weighed down by the immense responsibility of sorting through the details that invariably emerge at end of someone's life, Bree had forgotten all about that conversation—until she'd found the penny.

"So you brought it." Carmen picked up a knife and started to spread jam on a flaky pastry. "Is Venice the place?"

Bree squinted as she looked out into the morning sun once again. Finally, after a moment of consideration during which a table of six loud women broke out in gales of laughter and hooted over something one of them had said, she turned back to Carmen and focused her gaze.

"It is," she said. "Venice is *definitely* the place."

THE INFO SHEET THAT LUCY HANDED THEM ON THE WAY OUT OF THE restaurant had a list of local restaurants, major landmarks, times of special Carnival events, and walking directions to the local *mascareri* where they could buy a pre-made mask or help to design one of their own to wear as they roamed the streets amongst the other masked revelers.

"Should we get masks?" Carmen asked, consulting the sheet as they stood on the cobblestone street outside the hotel. "I mean, we should obviously have masks, right?" Her eyes followed two dark-haired, sleekly dressed men speaking Italian punctuated with hand gestures as they walked by, newspapers tucked under their arms.

They were clearly on their way to work, and Bree reached out to grab Carmen's arm to make sure she didn't follow along after them like a lost American puppy.

Bree took a sip of the coffee that she'd begged their waiter to put in a to-go cup; she was going to have to battle her jet lag one way or another. "Yes, we should absolutely have masks. Let's do that first, huh?"

With a last glance at the retreating figures of the dashing men on their morning commute to offices unknown, Carmen led the way through the streets of Venice. They marveled together at the way the February sun cast shadows and turned shaded side alleys into cold, dark passageways, while at the same time making the canals look like sparkling ribbons that ran alongside the streets and under the many bridges. Even early in the day, tourists and locals alike walked around in ornate, glittering, bejeweled masks of every color combination imaginable, and many people were dressed in costumes that harkened back to eighteenth century Venice, when people donned masks in order to mingle anonymously and to partake in mischief without being identified.

"Just wait till I catch a hot young guy in a mask and we rush off together without even speaking the same language or knowing anything about one another," Carmen said, looking around eagerly as she snapped photos with her phone.

"Sounds about right." Bree smiled wryly and tossed her empty coffee cup into a trash can. It didn't matter what continent they were on, Carmen was Carmen and men were fair game.

Standing near several small docked gondolas was a woman in a shiny gold lamé ballgown with an enormous bustle. Her tall, curly, powdered wig towered at least two feet above her head, and over her face she wore a mask covered in glittering gold butterflies. Bree glanced up at the wig and realized that the same gold butterflies had been turned into hair combs and were scattered throughout her curls as well. As a small crowd looked on, the woman acted out the opera playing from a speaker next to her, pantomiming all the feelings and emotions that went along with the words.

"This is wild," Carmen said, watching as a middle-aged man in jeans and a fanny pack dropped onto the cobblestones and laid on his stomach as he videotaped the performance from that lower angle. "Look at how old that church is!" She pointed at a stone chapel down the street. "And I want to find the *best* pizza for lunch—who cares if we just had breakfast!"

"Opera, buildings, pizza, hot men—I need a minute to catch up here," Bree said, putting a hand to her chest and bending forward theatrically like she was out of breath. "Just give me a second."

Bree stood up straight and breathed in deeply as she turned around in a slow circle and took it all in: people in half-masks that left their mouths visible; others in full, painted masks; some with just their eyes covered like Zorro. The sunlight glinted off of rhinestones and camera screens and canals, creating a swirl of light and color as Bree turned the full 360 degrees, face tipped up at the blue morning sky.

For a moment, before her senses returned and she remembered who she was and why she was in Venice, she imagined that hiding behind a mask might allow her to hide how hard this first trip out into the world without Kenny was for her. Maybe it would even allow her to become someone else entirely for the remainder of the trip.

But nothing could happen for Bree until she made good on her promise to Kenny. Not until she found a place to make the kind of wish that would be worthy of releasing the penny her husband had worn in his shoe. She needed it to be the kind of wish that would transform her life and her heart...the kind of wish that would make Kenny proud.

The kind of wish that might set her free.

7

FEBRUARY 12
VENICE, ITALY

"Hi!" Lucy felt tears spring to her eyes as Nick's face appeared on her phone screen. But that was ridiculous, she told herself. It had been just days since she'd left home, and while she saw Nick everyday, he wasn't her boyfriend or anything.

But still. There was his face and here were her tears.

"Hey!" Nick grinned at her widely and propped his phone up so that she was looking at him sideways. He rubbed his eyes.

"Oh no! You're sleeping, Nick," she said, feeling like a total moron. Of course he was sleeping—it was noon in Venice, so Lucy did a quick mental count—six a.m. on Amelia Island. "Did I wake you?"

"Only a half hour before my alarm. No big deal." Nick rolled onto his side and looked at the phone screen. "Sorry you're seeing me in bed, though."

Lucy felt a blush, an actual, honest to god blush, creep up her chest at the mention of the word "bed" from Nick. She had no idea why, because obviously he would have a bed and obviously he would sleep in it, but for some reason she felt as though she'd just climbed in next to him.

"Please, do not apologize," Lucy said quickly, trying to stop her train of thought before it ran away like a mischievous toddler let loose in a park. "How's Hemingway?"

"Hemmie? He's good," Nick said. His lazy smile and the way his hair stuck out all around his head on the pillow made Lucy feel hot in the cheeks again. "Hey, Hem!" he called out. Instantly, a blob of black fur pounced on the bed behind him and laid its snout on Nick's bare shoulder. "There he is."

Lucy smiled and her tears dried instantly. This picture right here (if she'd dared to take a screenshot of it—which she *didn't* dare) was the kind of image that went viral on Instagram and on every other app that women frequented. Handsome, sleepy, bare-chested man with a black lab? *Check, check, check, and YES, PLEASE*, said nearly every straight, red-blooded woman on planet Earth, and maybe even a few who didn't solely prefer men. Lucy kept her eyes trained on Nick's face and avoided looking at his exposed skin as much as possible.

"Where are you?" Nick asked, blinking a few times and scanning the screen as he tried to determine her whereabouts.

Lucy looked around and then back at Nick on the phone screen. "I'm sitting on the edge of a fountain on the Ponte di Rialto," she said, adjusting her AirPods and leaning to one side so that Nick could see the water spouting from the fountain just over her shoulder. "All the water in Venice is safe for drinking and there's plenty of it—"

"Which makes sense," Nick said, propping himself up on one elbow and letting his sheet fall away from his chest in the process. A tattoo of a daisy—a single, perfectly etched daisy—sat over his heart. Lucy hadn't known about the tattoo. "Given that Venice is built completely on water."

"Exactly. So people walk around with their own water bottles and just refill them all over the city," Lucy said, trying not to stare at his body.

"Have you been to the fountain of wine yet?"

"No, but I can promise you I *will* be going there. Every city should have its own fountain of wine."

There was a split-second pause as Nick reached over to pet Hemingway. "So what's up? Did you need me to swing by and water your plants or anything?"

"No, Lois is going to do all that," Lucy said, looking away from the phone. She focused on a family in colorful masks as they stopped and pulled out various water bottles to refill from the fountain behind her. "She's taking care of Joji and watching the house, yadda yadda yadda."

"Mmm," Nick said, looking at her intently. He seemed to be waiting for Lucy to divulge a reason for her call, but all of a sudden, she realized that her initial plan, which was to jokingly ask him if Amelia Island had floated away in her brief absence, might sound like an incredibly ridiculous reason for calling at six o'clock in the morning.

"Actually," Lucy took a deep breath. "I was wondering. Was it you who sent me the snow globe? Of Venice?"

A slow, guilty smile crept across Nick's face. "Yeah," he said, petting Hemingway's head next to him. "It was. I just wanted to get you something to commemorate the trip. I know this year is a big deal for you, and I felt really proud of you for pulling it off. You're so good at what you do that sometimes I forget you had a whole other life and career before this."

"Well, I haven't exactly pulled it off yet." Lucy blushed again. This time it wasn't from the heat of embarrassment, but rather from pleasure. Of all the people in her life, Nick perhaps knew the most about her struggles to find her footing on Amelia Island, get over the heartache she'd left behind in Buffalo, and wade through the nonsense that had come of her brief cohabitation with Katrina and her even briefer relationship with Charlie. "But thanks, Nick. That means a lot to me."

"You're welcome." Nick sat up fully, dragging the blanket with him so that it covered his body all the way up to his chest. "And now, I need to get ready for work. I've got to head over there to wait for the one lost tourist who might need directions to the beach, the one eighty-two-year-old man who isn't sure how to work his phone but assumes that because I'm 'a youngster' I probably know how every single brand of electronic device works, and maybe three women over the age of sixty who want to buy stamps."

"Don't forget about the Amazon guy," Lucy said. "You two seem to have a pretty deep relationship. But yikes." She cringed. "Is it that bad? Even during season?"

"Season" was essentially the time between October and April when what felt like every retiree in the country descended on the state of Florida, and it usually meant an uptick in business as well as a glut of humanity in every store, on every road, and on all the beaches. By and large, the locals of every city and community in Florida both grudgingly looked forward to the boom in business that came with the season, and violently abhorred the influx of oldsters who walked, drove, and did everything much more slowly than was absolutely necessary. Lucy herself had been guilty once or twice of barely disguised impatience as she stood behind someone in line at Publix and waited while they slowly wrote out an actual, honest to God *check* to pay for their groceries.

"Yeah, it's pretty slow," Nick said, motioning for Hemingway to hop off the bed.

"Maybe you should hang up a *Gone Fishin'* sign on the door and come to St. Barts with me next month." The words were out of Lucy's mouth before she could stop them.

"You think so?" Nick smiled. "Maybe I should. I could trade one island for another and get a change of scenery."

Lucy wasn't entirely sure that she meant for him to take her seriously so she quickly changed the subject.

"You need to get to work!" she said too forcefully. "I'll let you get up and make coffee and everything. Have a great day, and sorry again that I woke you."

"No worries. Life isn't the same in the old strip mall without you right next door. You can call, text, or email me anytime."

"But," Lucy said, pausing for dramatic effect, "can I fax you?"

Nick laughed loudly. "Sure you can. Just wait for that screeching fax sound, okay?"

"Bye, Nick," Lucy said, smiling at him one last time.

"*Arrivederci*, Lucy."

8

FEBRUARY 12

VENICE, ITALY

"How about the canal that runs under the Bridge of Sighs?" Carmen offered. She was flipping through a guidebook as Bree leaned on a railing, watching people board a gondola with a singing gondolier. Much to her amusement, the gondolier was happily chortling "That's Amore" in a voice that sounded surprisingly like Dean Martin.

"The Bridge of Sighs," Bree repeated, her eyes glazed and faraway as the breeze lifted her dark hair from her shoulders. "That sounds romantic."

"The actual bridge looks totally enclosed in these photos, so I don't think we can get up there and toss it from that part, but there's an open walkway that runs parallel to the bridge and we can definitely stand there if you want."

Bree pushed away from the railing and gathered herself. She looked at Carmen squarely. "Look, Carm. I know this isn't why you came to Venice, and I don't want you to spend your first full day in this beautiful city trying to help me find a bridge from which to carry out my somewhat depressing task. So I hereby release you from this project, and I promise I can get it handled on my own. I've got this." Bree held up a hand like she was swearing on a bible in a courtroom.

"Hey." Carmen closed the guidebook and looked at Bree seriously. "Don't you say that. I'm here for *you*. This entire trip is *our* trip, yes, but it's also your first trip after losing Kenny, and I don't care if we spend the entire vacation sharing memories, crying, or looking for a good spot to pitch your damn penny into the water. You hear me?"

Bree's eyes welled with tears. Rather than speak, she just nodded.

"Okay, now let's head over to the Bridge of Sighs and see if we like it." Carmen shoved the guidebook into her oversized shoulder bag and led the way.

The canal that ran beneath the footbridge and then under the Bridge of Sighs was emerald green. Bree stopped and leaned over the railing again, watching the soft ripple of the water being churned by gondolas. The canal was lined by ornate carved stone buildings on both sides, onto which the water lapped noisily.

Carmen walked all the way over the footbridge, leaving Bree to assess the spot and to think for a minute. When she turned and walked back, Bree had both hands on the handrail with its baroque miniature columns. She looked over at Carmen and gave a single nod.

"This is it? You sure?" Carmen leaned against the columns with one denim-clad hip. She brushed a hand over her thick curls and narrowed her eyes at Bree. "We can keep looking and make sure you aren't being hasty. There's absolutely no reason to be in a hurry here."

Bree shook her head and glanced around. Any place she chose would be both the best and the worst place to do this, and leaving the task for later was just inviting heartache to overtake the trip. "I'm sure. This is the spot."

Carmen inhaled and exhaled. She scratched her chin and looked as though she wanted to say more, but then didn't. "Okay. I got you, girl. What do you want me to do?"

Bree unzipped her crossbody purse and pulled out a little pink sachet. She untied it and tipped the opening over her hand, releasing the penny into her palm. The midday sun glinted off the copper.

"Will you go over there and just take video of me making the wish and tossing the coin?" Bree pointed at a spot to her right.

"You want me to take video?" Carmen frowned. It was an unusual request from her friend, who normally wasn't even thrilled to be photographed.

Bree nodded, already distracted by the task at hand.

"Okay. Of course I will." Carmen took several steps back and got her phone out. She set it to video mode and hit record, waiting for Bree to do her thing.

Bree inhaled deeply. She clutched the penny in her hand as she closed her eyes and leaned forward over the water. This was it. A year of waking up in the middle of the night and rolling over to Kenny's side of the bed, still thinking he might be there. A year of feeling guilty if she so much as envisioned a future without him. A year of wondering why them...why him...why now. How come they couldn't have had forty or fifty more years together? And now she had to make a wish and begin the long, sad process of letting him go.

With another deep inhale and exhale, Bree tried to imagine what Kenny might want for her. The sun warmed the top of her head as she felt the smooth edges of the coin in her palm. He'd want her to be happy, of course. And he'd want her to feel free to live her life at some point. There was no way he expected her to stay suspended in amber forever, thirty-three years old and mourning his loss eternally. Bree knew that. She cleared her throat and a thought began to form in her head; the beginnings of a wish worth making.

Unbeknownst to Bree, a group of joggers were making their way towards the footbridge at that exact moment, cutting through knots of people in masks and costumes, and as they did, one of the joggers accidentally misjudged his footing and did a near-miss with an older woman who'd stopped to photograph the Bridge of Sighs. In the nick of time, he dodged the woman and her camera, but went shoulder first into Bree's back, giving her a shove that both knocked the wind out of her and dislodged the penny from her grasp.

Gasping in surprise, Bree caught herself on the railing with both hands.

"*Mi dispiace*," the man said, breathing heavily and already scanning the crowd for his jogging partners. He ran off without another word.

Bree barely clocked any of it. The second the penny left her clutches, her eyes were on it. She watched its slow descent through the air as it flipped head over tails, catching bits of sunlight as it succumbed to the pull of gravity.

Somewhere between the penny's rotation and the glimmer of light on copper, the stern of a gondola had slipped into view as it traveled beneath the footbridge on its way toward the Bridge of Sighs.

"Oh," Bree said softly, already understanding what was about to happen. She watched as the rest of the gondola—its gondolier, its passengers—slid out from under the footbridge. A word began to form on her lips as the penny continued falling, but she wasn't sure what that word should be. How to shout out in a split second to a group of strangers who might not even speak English that her late husband's good luck coin was about to land in their midst and that she desperately needed it back?

But there wasn't time anyway. Before the words could spill from her lips, Bree watched as the penny landed with a *plonk* on the dark, curly head of a man in a navy blue sweater. He looked up, surprise etched all over his handsome face as his hand raked through his curls, seeking out the offending missile.

"That's my—" Bree called, one hand reaching out as if he might be able to throw it back to her.

In response, the man opened his hand and looked down at the coin in his palm. A slow smile spread across his face and he rose to his feet in the middle of the gondola, holding the penny up with a smile of victory.

"No..." Bree whispered, hand still outstretched as the gondola meandered onward, its metal prow winking at her in the same rays of sunlight that her penny had. "No."

With an exaggerated back and forth wave of his arm, the man held the penny in the air once again, then sat down just as the boat drifted under the Bridge of Sighs.

BREE AND CARMEN RAN DOWN THE STREET, SHOUTING AT ONE ANOTHER and weaving between pedestrians as they approached the spot on the edge of the fountain where Lucy was still sitting. She'd just ended her call with Nick and was putting her AirPods back in their case when the commotion of Carmen and Bree yelling loudly got her attention.

"Hey! Ladies!" Lucy stood up and planted herself firmly in front of Bree, who came to a halt, looking absolutely harried. "Is everything okay? Are you being mugged in broad daylight?"

"Yes!" Bree shouted, grabbing Lucy by both elbows and giving her a little shake. "I've been robbed!"

Carmen slowed to a stop and bent forward slightly at the waist to catch her breath. "No," she wheezed. "We are *not* being mugged."

"My penny!" Bree wailed. "It's gone and the boat went that way." She pointed feebly at the canal as it emerged from behind a row of buildings. And then another gondola followed. And another.

"Your penny?" Lucy put the straps of her canvas bag over one shoulder and looked from one woman to the other. "You lost a penny?" She'd put her puzzle-solving skills to work hundreds of times during the course of her former career to help resolve the unusual circumstances of any number of deaths, but she wasn't sure she'd be able to find a penny in a foreign city.

Carmen stood upright and gave herself two more breaths before explaining. "Bree's husband kept a penny in his shoe on their wedding day for good luck. His last wish was for her to take it somewhere interesting and make a wish with it, which she was *about* to do—"

"When a jackass jogger bumped me," Bree cut in, "and I dropped the penny. It fell into a gondola and hit some guy on the head."

Lucy made a pained face. "Okay. I'm seeing the importance of the penny more clearly."

"And he grabbed it," Bree went on with a touch of madness in her voice, "and *held it in the air* like he'd won a prize or something. My penny! He held it up like he was declaring victory. And now he's got it and I don't know where his gondola was going and if I don't get it back I'll never be able to make my wish and then—"

Carmen put her arms around her best friend and immediately shut off the flow of words. "Honey. You're getting hysterical. I'm gonna hold you in this bear hug until you can get yourself right. Just take a deep, calming breath, okay?"

Lucy fully expected Bree to get angry or to push Carmen away and keep ranting, but instead, she took the breath as instructed. She centered herself. And then a sense of calm appeared to wash over her. It was kind of magical to watch.

"Okay," Lucy said once they'd both been quiet for a moment. "So it landed in a gondola. I can see how that would upset you." She wracked her brain for any ideas that might pop up to help them track down the lucky penny, but she absolutely did not want to say anything that might upset Bree again.

"Hey," Carmen said, taking a tentative step away from her best friend. Bree remained calm as she tugged at the sleeves of her own sweater and rearranged her hair and her purse, which had gotten jumbled during her fast run through the streets of Venice. "I have an idea." As she spoke, Carmen pulled her phone out of her back pocket and held it up. "I took video of the whole thing."

"Oh!" Bree's face came to life again as she lunged for the phone. "I totally forgot! Do you think you got him on video?"

"Let's see." Carmen unlocked her phone and found the video, then hit play as the three women huddled around the screen.

An image popped up of Bree with the wind lifting her hair as she leaned slightly over the railing and looked down at the canal. People came and went around her, oblivious to the fact that a jet-lagged American woman was about to take a monumental step in her life by making good on a promise to her late husband.

They watched Bree stand and think for what felt like an inordinately long amount of time until the jogger suddenly came into frame and bumped into her from behind. With a sharp gasp, Bree pitched forward and let go of the coin, which was too small to be visible in the video. Carmen and Lucy both leaned in closer to see what happened next.

Without realizing it, Carmen had rushed closer to Bree, still holding her phone out, still recording. In doing so, she'd gotten the unlucky head of the man in the gondola, and as he looked up, Carmen had jostled her phone slightly, catching his surprised face for just a second before the lens of the camera skittered away and landed on the feet of the people walking past Bree and Carmen.

"That was him? Was that him?" Lucy looked back and forth between Bree and Carmen.

"Yep," Carmen confirmed. "That was him. The Hot Penny Thief."

"I mean, he *was* good looking," Lucy agreed.

Bree stood there shaking her head. "Fine," she said, clearly annoyed. "He was cute, but he canceled out my wish. I wonder if that means he gets all of my good luck? Or if I get bad luck for seven years or something?"

Lucy and Carmen made eye contact and exchanged a look. "I don't think there's really a precedent for this situation, girl," Carmen said. "So let's not jump down that particular rabbit hole just yet."

"But Venice is totally accessible," Lucy piped up. "You can wander the streets and museums and canals and try to spot him. Maybe he put the penny in his pocket and he'll give it back as soon as you guys find each other?"

"Or maybe he tossed it in the canal and made a wish of his own." Bree looked sick at this thought.

"Okay." Carmen clapped her hands together. She was louder than she needed to be, but it got Bree's attention. "First things first. We are going to get our masks. Then we're going to wander the streets all afternoon and keep our eyes peeled for this guy. Got it?"

"Can you take a screenshot of his face?" Lucy pointed at Carmen's phone, which she still held in her hand. "And text it to me? Then I can look for him too. I'm good at focusing on details."

This seemed to get Bree's attention. "Oh, that's a great idea, Lucy. Thank you. To both of you," she said, blinking back tears. "I know this is crazy and I don't want to drag you two into my drama, but..."

"You need that penny," Carmen said softly. "I know. I get it."

Lucy nodded, understanding immediately, though she'd only known Bree for about fifteen hours. "We'll do our best," she said, reaching out and putting a hand on Bree's arm. She gave it a light squeeze.

The fountain behind them roared, and people edged in around the three women to fill water bottles and to run their fingers through the cool rush of water.

Carmen and Lucy made quick work of getting a clear screenshot of the man's face and sharing it with one another, and then Lucy gathered her things and said she needed to get back to the hotel to double-check the various events for that evening.

"Let me know if you find him!" Lucy called out with a wave as she hurried across the cobblestones in her flat boots.

Because Lucy had shed most of her heavy winter gear before departing for warm, sunny Florida, Venice in February had necessitated a few purchases: a black turtleneck sweater; an overcoat; a pair of comfortable, knee-high suede boots for walking. Since starting the travel agency, her normal uniform had become some combination of sundress and sandals, but she was a wool and cashmere girl at heart, and she felt like herself again in her new clothes.

So far, being thousands of miles from home and steering the party boat for twenty strangers wasn't nearly as scary as she'd imagined it might be, and all in all, she was feeling pretty confident about the whole thing. For years, she'd kept a collection of articles, images, and words that she'd cut out of magazines tacked to a bulletin board in her kitchen, eyeballing it over a first cup of coffee before heading out into the dark, cold morning to identify yet another sad cause of death. On her vision board had been photos of white sandy beaches, European landmarks, the pyramids. She'd always known that someday, somehow she'd get to see the world. All it had taken was packing up her medical degree, enlisting her Aunt Sharon in her mother's care, and diving headfirst into the unknown.

The hard part for Lucy had been leaving her mother and convincing herself that it was in the best interest of *both* of them.

Things had been challenging with her mother for a long time, because her mom had suffered from agoraphobia for decades, and the fact that she wouldn't even leave her house in Buffalo to do her own grocery shopping was something that Lucy struggled with, and it had recently been compounded by a diagnosis of early-onset dementia. That had made leaving Buffalo even harder for Lucy, but it had also made it imperative. She often wondered whether it was somehow genetic: if she didn't break free and live her life, would it pass seamlessly from mother to daughter? Would she eventually just hole up in her own house with a cat or two and a failing memory and insist that the world didn't exist beyond her own front door? She didn't know anything for sure, but she'd known that somehow she had to prove to herself that her mother's curse wasn't necessarily *her* curse, and that the world she'd pushed aside while she finished medical school and started her career was still out there.

Lucy switched her bag from one shoulder to the other and watched as two little boys in sparkly black eye masks took turns leaping down three steps at a time in front of an old church. She smiled at a woman with a slightly hunched back as she sat near the boys and watched them play.

It was a nice contrast to the thoughts of her mother; she'd found that no matter how hard she tried to live—truly live—the guilt followed her everywhere. Leaving her mother's daily care to her aunt and a cast of paid professionals wasn't something she'd taken lightly, but she'd spent long, hard years dealing with the agoraphobia and its inherent limitations on her mother. Leaving when she had had somehow felt like the only way not to drown.

She still felt a lingering happiness after her short chat with Nick and Hemingway, and there were plenty of other things to do today. Not to mention the fact that she was going to scan every crowd for the face of the cute man who'd inadvertently caught the lucky penny of her new friend Bree.

Lucy made her way through the streets of Venice with her head held high. Her strides were long, and her mood was light. She felt like Mary Tyler Moore in the opening credits of *The Mary Tyler Moore*

Show until she noticed that people were looking at her with amused and sympathetic smiles.

Lucy glanced down at her black sweater; her grin faded when she realized that at some point, a wayward pigeon must have flown by and left a streak of white goop right down the middle of her not-very-ample chest.

"Dammit," she said to herself, pulling the black fabric away from her body as she assessed the damage to her new sweater.

"Is good luck. Is *very* good luck," an old man with a thick Italian accent said with a wink as he walked past Lucy.

"Right," she said to herself, blowing out a breath. "It's good luck."

9

FEBRUARY 12

VENICE, ITALY

I t was finally evening of the longest day that Bree had lived through in a long time. She'd gone way past exhaustion at dinner and decided to trickle water over the dumpster fire that was currently her brain by downing Diet Cokes one after the other.

"You're a little jittery there, girl." Carmen took her by the hand and led her through the darkened streets. They passed under strings of hanging Edison bulbs, pausing to watch men and women dressed in intricate, eye-catching Carnival costumes in a rainbow of colors.

"I drank a lot of Diet Coke," Bree admitted, letting Carmen drag her past three men in black capes and eye masks, each with a well-groomed mustache. In perfect harmony, they sang "God Only Knows" by the Beach Boys while a crowd of masked revelers looked on, some swaying to the song. This spectacle of handsome men harmonizing in the cool Venetian night air was the perfect mixture of magic to stop Carmen in her tracks.

"Oh," Carmen said, her mouth forming a perfect O as she readjusted her *colombina* mask, which was a gorgeous, bejeweled creation that covered only her eyes and tied at the back of her head. "This is lovely."

"Carm," Bree sighed, pushing her own mask just a fraction of an inch higher on her nose. They'd chosen their face coverings together that afternoon at the *mascareri,* and while it felt festive to wear, Bree was constantly lifting hers to scan the crowds around them. "The Penny Pincher didn't have any facial hair. None of these guys are him, unless he's raging with so much testosterone that he was able to grow a full mustache between noon and nine p.m."

Carmen's eyes were trained adoringly on the three well-built men in slim-cut black pants. One of them swirled his cape theatrically as he locked his gaze on Carmen.

"Oooh, I think he likes me," she said to Bree, nudging her with an elbow. "Do you think I should ask him to have a drink after he's done performing?"

Bree shrugged. "Yeah, I guess. I don't see why not." She wanted to stamp her foot and remind Carmen that they were on a *mission,* but the adult part of her that understood how much Carmen needed a vacation too stopped her from trying to pull all the attention back to the issue at hand. And a little part of her wanted to try out being more like Carmen for once. To take a risk—a leap of faith—and let destiny and chance take over. "Maybe he knows a good place to hang out around here."

"Good thinking." Carmen moved closer to the singing trio. As soon as they took a break to bask in the applause from the gathered crowd for a minute, she walked right up to them and leaned in close to the one on the end, resting her hand in the crook of his elbow as she spoke directly into his ear.

Bree blew out a long sigh. She was tired and she could easily have just gone back to the hotel to sleep, but surely the Coin Catcher was out roaming the streets of the city, waiting to be found, and she wouldn't rest until she'd tracked him down.

"Okay!" Carmen was out of breath when she returned to Bree's side, eyes dancing behind her mask. "He says there's a private party going on a few blocks from here, and I got the scoop on how to get in."

"A private party? For what?"

Carmen made a face. "Who cares? It's exclusive, it's not for the generic masses, and we're in. All we have to do is show up in our masks and say that 'Giacomo eats clams fresh from the ocean.'"

Bree looked at her incredulously. "Seriously?"

"It's a code, like 'The Eagle has landed.'"

"Ohhh, gotcha. Okay. Giacomo eats clams. For sure." Bree slumped against a cold stone wall and tried to summon some deep reserve of strength from within. She had no idea what well of energy Carmen dipped her cup in to drink from, but she needed some of whatever fueled her friend.

"You okay, girl?" Carmen put her hands on both of Bree's shoulders and focused in on her eyes. "Seriously, we can just forget about Giacomo and head back to the hotel if you want. It's only day one and you've barely slept. I don't want you to overdo it right off the top."

Bree gave a soft laugh. "You haven't slept much either," she argued. People wandered all over the streets wearing their most elaborate costumes and masks, laughing and talking as they took in Venice at night.

"Well, we both know I was born to party. You, not so much." Carmen smiled wryly. "Love you anyway, though." She wasn't wrong; they'd met at a college party and hit it off instantly, and ever since that fateful evening Carmen had been the one dragging Bree from one adventure to the next. Bree never minded basking in the sunshine that Carmen created, and her own calm presence kept them both grounded through several of Carmen's wilder romantic escapades, an ill-advised move Carmen had made to LA after college to find an acting agent, and any number of the other dramas that life had thrown their way.

Bree pushed herself away from the wall and shook off the feelings of fatigue as best she could. "I can do this," she said with certainty. "I definitely can."

Carmen laced her fingers through Bree's and gave her hand a squeeze. "Alright, girl. Then let's go check out this clambake, shall we?"

A KNOCK ON AN OLD WOODEN DOOR THAT LOOKED AS IF IT WERE SIZED for much smaller people gave way to a loud dance party with flashing lights that changed colors every thirty seconds or so. Bree trailed in after Carmen, who had shouted at the masked man at the door that Giacomo ate his clams fresh from the sea, but since the man was clearly several drinks into his evening already, or maybe he was hopped up on something more pharmaceutical, all he'd really done was wave them in and point in the direction of the blue neon-lit bar.

"What can I get you?" Carmen said loudly, enunciating her words to be heard over the thrum of pulsing music. She looked around to see what everyone else was drinking. "Beer?"

"I don't care. Anything is fine!" Bree shouted back, tugging on Carmen's arm to pull her closer. At first glance, everyone there was masked and dressed in black, and from the way they danced, she could tell they were all young; most likely thirty and under. They honestly weren't much younger than Bree and Carmen, but something about the way they danced and moved around, loose limbed and unencumbered, made Bree feel out of her element. World weary. Like none of these people had yet to experience the weight of commitment, love, and deep loss. It felt like a vast ocean separated Bree from other people of her own generation. It couldn't have been true though; people other than her suffered their own tragedies, but it was easier sometimes to feel alone in her pain. Their carefree smiles and easy laughter were like salt in her wounds.

"Hey," Bree said to Carmen as she turned to the bar. "Do you think we really belong here? Like, are we too old?"

"What?" Carmen leaned in closer. "I couldn't hear you!"

"Do you think we're too *old* for this party?"

Carmen still wasn't comprehending. She frowned and put a hand to her ear.

"Never mind," Bree said, waving a hand. "A beer is good." She stood in place, conspicuously not dancing as she waited for Carmen to come back with two Heinekens. The song that was playing was a remix of a classic 80s song that she loved, so Bree bobbed her head lightly as she glanced around.

"Hello." A short, muscular man in a mask and a sweaty black t-shirt stood in front of Bree, holding a bottle of beer to his chest as he eyed her hungrily.

"No thank you," Bree said without hesitation. She turned to find Carmen and nearly slammed face first into her friend. Carmen thrust a beer in her direction. "Thanks. Let's move around."

Since conversation was nearly impossible, Bree led the way up the spiral staircase in the center of the room—was it a bar? A town-house? A business? Late at night and with only the dizzying display of flashing lights to guide them through the mass of sweaty bodies, the space could have been anything, really—and they ended up on the second floor, looking down at the teeming mass of humanity as it surged and moved to the beat of the music.

"Where's your Beach Boy?" Bree asked at a more conversational volume, now that they were far from the speakers and the deejay.

Carmen's eyes scanned the crowd below. "He wasn't even Italian," she said as she searched for her caped crooner. "As soon as he started talking, I realized he was German."

"Bummer."

Carmen laughed, immediately getting the joke. "I know, I know. I've already had a German or two, and I really need to find some more diversity if I'm going to complete my Men of the World Challenge."

Bree rolled her eyes and put the bottle of beer to her lips, though she knew that doing anything more than taking baby sips of it would render her totally useless and that she'd end up curled in the fetal position on a banquette, sleeping till morning while Carmen made out with the German guy in the bathroom of this place.

"You do know that there are something like 195 independent countries in the world, right?" Bree dropped her chin and looked at Carmen with disbelief. "There's no way you can find a man from each of them. Not in this lifetime."

"You wanna bet? Here, hold my beer." Carmen passed her bottle to Bree and hurried toward the staircase, shimmying down and weaving through the group of women who were currently on their way up. Bree watched over the railing, a bottle of beer in each hand, as Carmen made her way to the dance floor. She threw her arms in the air as she blended into the melee, spinning in circles and letting her curls fly. Her hips shook and her body swayed with abandon. Within seconds, no fewer than four men had surrounded her, moving alongside her as if she were dancing with them and not simply adjacent to them, and one even pulled up behind her, setting his hands on Carmen's hips and moving in time to the music like they'd come to the party together.

"Damn it. She's actually going to do it," Bree said to herself, shaking her head. She gave in and took a long swig of her beer as she held Carmen's bottle in the other hand. "Somehow, some way, she's going to find a dude from every country." It amazed her, and while she loved Carmen's zest for life, she had no designs on conquering men the way her friend did. But she would have taken just a sliver of the self-assurance that Carmen walked through the world wearing like a perfectly tailored suit.

Carmen looked up just then, waving her arms excitedly as she spotted Bree. The guy behind her looked up too, trying to follow her gaze. It was then that Bree saw his eyes and his dark curls and his navy blue sweater, and even with the mask on she knew—she *knew*—it was the guy who'd caught her penny.

Bree set the beers on the nearest empty table and hurried over to the stairs, shouldering her way through five or six people all shouting and laughing in Italian.

"Excuse me," she said, trying to get two people to move aside. "Sorry, can I get by?" Bree glanced in the direction of the dance floor, the view of which was partially obscured by the staircase. She had to get down there. Carmen was dancing with him and she had no idea that Bree's penny was most likely in the pocket of the guy who was just inches from grinding up against her.

Bree tried waving again, but Carmen had gone back to dancing, eyes closed, possessed by the music like no one was watching.

The guy behind Carmen cast a glance in Bree's direction and she yanked off her mask and narrowed her eyes to get a better look. It was definitely him, but now that he wasn't in a gondola, she could see that in addition to the well-cut navy sweater, he was also wearing a pair of jeans that reminded her distinctly of President Obama's infamous belted Dad Jeans and a pair of too-white sneakers. Was this look ironic, or was her International Penny Thief just a big goof in denim and tennies? In spite of herself, Bree almost laughed.

Once she reached the stairs, she grabbed the handrail and tried to stick close to the side of the steps so as not to get caught in the flow of upstream traffic. The rapidly changing colored lights were dizzying as Bree made her way down the spiral staircase, and with each turn, Carmen would come in and out of view until Bree finally reached the dance floor. She nearly broke into a run to get to Carmen.

"Carm!" Bree called out urgently, feeling herself being pulled away from Carmen by the flow of dancing bodies around her. "Hey! Where did he go?" she yelled, looking everywhere for the guy in the Dad Jeans.

She finally got to Carmen and put her face right up close to her best friend's ear. "Carmen!" she pleaded. "Where did he go? Where is that guy?"

Carmen stopped dancing and looked right into Bree's eyes. "Who? Which guy?" she shouted over the music.

But it was no use. Bree turned and looked at the rapturous, sweaty faces of the masked dancers around them as the lights flashed yellow, then blue, then purple, then green. None of the faces were the one she was looking for. He was already gone.

10

FEBRUARY 13
VENICE, ITALY

"Hi!" Lucy said, waving both hands at Bree and Carmen when they stepped out of the elevator and into the lobby the next morning. "Did you two sleep well?"

Carmen yawned.

"We slept pretty well," Bree said, looking somewhat fresher than the day before. She'd gotten up early that morning and showered, flat-ironed her hair, and chosen an oversized, lipstick red sweater and a pair of slim, white jeans. Her Carnival mask was in her bag, and she was ready for coffee and breakfast.

"What's on the docket for the day? Are you joining the tour at St. Mark's Basilica?" Lucy pulled a sheet of paper off the pile in her arm and handed it to Bree, who was clearly the one taking the lead that morning. Carmen had yet to crack a smile. In fact, she reminded Lucy of a coworker she'd had in Buffalo—a grouchy older pathologist named Ed who'd refused to speak out loud until ten o'clock, at which point he'd turn to Lucy and growl, "Now that I've had my coffee, you wanna introduce me to the dead guy on your table?"

"I think so. And we wanted to look into the boat tour to Murano and Burano at some point." Her eyes flicked in Carmen's direction. "But maybe not today."

Lucy nodded knowingly. A woman who also had the distinct look of someone in need of a strong cup of coffee walked over and held out a hand without speaking. "Good morning, Mrs. Severson," Lucy said to her, passing one of her printed pages to the woman. "I hope you're having a good time so far."

"So far, so good," Mrs. Severson said, immediately folding the paper in half fanning herself with it. "But being old and out of shape is gonna kill me. You girls enjoy being young while you can, you hear?"

Bree smiled kindly and watched as Mrs. Severson disappeared through the open doors to the dining room.

Lucy was dressed in a denim jumpsuit that morning with ankle boots and a bun on top of her head. She'd jammed a sharp yellow pencil through the knot of hair. "Anyway," she said, turning back to Bree and Carmen. "Have you had any luck tracking down Mr. Gondola?"

Carmen made a noise that sounded half like a groan of pain, and half like a plea for mercy. Lucy shot her a concerned look. The doctor in her instantly started to calculate and add up what she was seeing: grayish pallor, dehydrated skin around the eyes...official diagnosis: too much alcohol and not enough sleep.

"Don't worry, she's fine," Bree said, watching Carmen warily after catching Lucy's assessing gaze. "The past couple of days have finally caught up to her, but she'll live."

"I don't mean to be pushy, but I'd match her coffee with water ounce for ounce, and if she needs to go upstairs for a nap, let her." Lucy shot Carmen a sympathetic look. "I've been where you are, and it's no fun."

Carmen mumbled something semi-coherent.

"And you know what?" Bree went on, smiling brightly to make up for Carmen's dourness. "We did see him. Last night we got into some weird, exclusive party, and I swear I saw him on the dance floor, trying to grind on Carmen like an international creeper."

"He had a mask on, Bree," Carmen said, with a warning in her voice. "And he wasn't grinding on me, there were a million people dancing together, and he was just one of the bodies out there. I don't want you to get too worked up every time you see a guy with curly dark hair. It might not have even been him."

"It *was* him," Bree said seriously, turning to face Carmen. "It was definitely him."

Carmen held up both hands and closed her eyes briefly. "You're right. It probably was."

It was clear that Bree and Carmen weren't quite on the same page yet that morning.

"So, St. Mark's will be fun," Lucy said, giving them both a winning smile. "And there are several cute restaurants in the area, as well as lots of shopping." The months of research she'd done before the trip were paying off with each person she talked to, as she was able to confidently point out landmarks on maps and make suggestions like she'd spent plenty of time exploring Venice with her own two feet rather than via YouTube videos and various travel websites.

"You know," Carmen said darkly, folding her arms across her chest as she stared straight at Lucy. "You're really good at this." Bree looked at Carmen with a warning in her eyes. "You're perky like a cruise director."

"She means that in the nicest way," Bree said, reaching out a tentative hand like she was going to set it on Lucy's arm. "You're amazing at making everyone feel like they're part of a group without forcing us to absolutely do group things."

Lucy kept her smile pasted on firmly. "Thanks. I mean, I want people to have a home base and someone to turn to in case they feel like doing something pre-planned or whatever, but at the same time, going on vacation is such a personal experience. This way you feel like you know people in Venice, but you're under no obligation to hang out with them if you don't want to."

"I think it's a great set up, Lucy," Bree assured her, taking Carmen by the arm firmly. "We're going to get some breakfast here. Maybe we'll see you at St. Mark's."

With a bit more force than necessary, Bree steered Carmen in the direction of the smell of coffee. "What is your problem?" she hissed. "I could tell you were grumpy when we woke up, but are you really slinging insults at Lucy? She's been nothing but nice to us."

Carmen pouted for a second. "I didn't mean to. I guess I'm just tired." Her arms dropped from their defensive folded position and her shoulders slumped. "Do you think I should go back and apologize? I'm not really bringing my A-game yet today, but I don't want to come across as a total ass."

"It's fine. I think we're okay with Lucy. Just be extra nice and give her the *real* Carmen treatment next time we see her, not this cranky, pissed off version, alright?" Bree shook her head disapprovingly.

"You're right. Get some coffee in me. Then we'll go attack this city again. I think I'm also feeling kind of bad that I had your guy that close on the dance floor and I let him get away."

"Carm—you couldn't have known. Come on."

"Well, he'd better watch out today," Carmen said, picking a table and pulling out the chair. "Because there is *no way* he's getting away from us a second time."

NORMALLY LUCY HAD MUCH THICKER SKIN. A MILDLY SNARKY COMMENT from a tired traveler shouldn't throw her off as much as it had when Carmen had called her a cruise director. In her former life she'd been accused by families of covering up a loved one's murder by filing her official pathologist's report with a final ruling of suicide (she'd found that no one liked to believe someone they cared about had made that final and irreversible decision), and she'd been called on to oversee some horrifically gruesome things. So this should be nothing, but the fact that she was doing something totally new to her, and doing it on foreign soil, had made her feel extra vulnerable. She didn't have a pair of scrubs, a face mask, gloves, booties, and a medical degree to use as her armor, and instead she was all out there, just herself, smiling away and hoping that people were enjoying the trip.

Instead of letting it get under her skin and dominate her thoughts all day, she'd forced herself to meet up with the people who'd signed on for the St. Mark's tour after breakfast, and with a smile planted firmly on her face, she'd walked through the streets, making small talk with Mrs. Severson and her traveling companion, a loud, raspy-voiced woman named Marge who had long ago parted ways with her bra and any other lingering inhibitions.

"Lucy," Marge said once they were inside the museum, her voice booming and echoing around the room as they looked at the four bronze horses stolen from Istanbul and brought home from the Crusades. "A man is a lot like a horse," she went on, leaning her weight on a bedazzled cane that sparkled under the overhead museum lighting. Her jowls shuddered slightly as she spoke. "He can be broken and he can be tamed, but there always, *always* needs to be trust in the relationship. He has to trust that you'll feed him and care for him, and you have to trust that he won't spook and run away. You understand?"

Lucy's phone buzzed in her pocket and she was desperate to excuse herself and answer it, but instead she nodded, looking thoughtful. "I do," she said. "How do you and Mrs. Severson know each other?" She made an attempt to shift the conversation.

"Diane?" Marge snorted. "We drove school buses together for twenty-six years. She's like a sister to me."

At the mention of her name, Diane Severson emerged from the ladies' room and made her way over to where Lucy and Marge were standing. "Damn bathroom was out of soap," she grumbled. "You telling tales about me, Marge?"

Marge gave a hearty laugh and tapped her cane on the floor. "Damn straight I would, if there was a single interesting thing to share about an old gal like you."

Diane's face softened, and as Lucy watched the two old friends, she could see a girlishness in their exchange. For a moment it made her miss the friendships and work relationships she'd had in Buffalo, but just as quickly as the feeling had come on, it passed. As she often did, she reminded herself that Amelia Island was home now, and that she was forming bonds there and creating a life that would soon feel like it truly belonged to her.

"The truth is, I was giving this young thing a bit of advice about men," Marge said.

"Oh lord." Diane rolled her eyes. "She sleeps with three men her entire life and suddenly she thinks she's Elizabeth Taylor."

"Hey, just because you saved yourself for Dwayne and then closed up shop when he died doesn't mean the rest of us are opposed to a little slap and tickle, you know?"

"Oh *lord*!" Diane said again, this time with a cackle that caught Lucy by surprise. So far on the trip she'd pegged Mrs. Severson as nothing more than a grumpy Boomer with a pre-packaged complaint for every situation, but seeing her with Marge was a bit of a revelation. Rather than just harrumphing about things and asking curt questions, she seemed somehow lighter. More human.

"Now listen here, Lucy," Marge said, inching closer and tapping her cane again loudly to make sure she had the floor and the attention of everyone within a thirty foot radius. "After my husband passed, I slept with his brother."

Lucy choked on her own spit, then pounded her chest to clear her windpipe. "Excuse me," she said, gasping a little. "I'm sorry—go on."

"Larry wasn't as handsome as Bill, that's for damn sure, but I knew him, and he was kind, and—to be perfectly honest—built much like his brother." She shrugged. "So it was an easy way for me to get back on the horse, so to speak." With this, Marge raised her cane and pointed it at the horses for emphasis.

"God almighty," Diane said, shaking her head and acting like she'd never heard this story, though Lucy would have bet both her business and her bungalow on the fact that Diane had lived through the whole thing and then heard it retold at least a thousand times.

"Anyway, Larry was a decent lover," Marge went on loudly, "but then I met Jim. A younger man. Which I think makes me a bit of a cougar, doesn't it?" she asked, giving Lucy a wicked look that was filled with pride.

"I guess it does," Lucy agreed, suddenly remembering the pencil shoved in her hair. She reached up and pulled it out of her bun, letting her hair fall loose around her shoulders.

"Jim was impaired," Diane interrupted, shaking her head. "He was ten years younger than Marge, and some people say his mama dropped him on his head one too many times as a baby."

"But when I saw him out mowing the lawn of the church..." Marge said, licking her lips for emphasis. "All I'm saying is that he was as hungry for love as I was. And he wasn't *that* impaired," she said, giving Diane a withering look.

"Well," Lucy said, dropping the pencil from her hair into her purse and pulling her phone out of her back pocket. "All I can say is *wow*. This has been...wow." She glanced at her phone screen with a studied frown. "Oh, I'm sorry ladies—it looks like I missed a call from the hotel." She nodded at the doorway and beat a hasty retreat for the exit as she put her phone to her ear and pretended to return a call.

In truth, all she'd missed was a text from Dev, which made her heart race a little as she opened her message app and read it:

Hey, Miss Adventure. Things aren't the same around here without you. How's Venice? If you don't come back, I'll officially consider your tab at Beans & Sand closed, and will have to track you down through a collections agency to make sure I get my $32.87.

Lucy's face was plastered with a huge grin as she stood in the mercifully quiet room beyond the bronze horses and read Dev's words to herself a few times.

But seriously, his second text said, *I was just thinking of you and hoping that everything was going well.*

Much like talking to Nick, reading a text from Dev filled Lucy with a flush of pleasure that she tried to tie exclusively to the fact that they both represented the familiar; they were a part of her everyday life. But a little part of her knew that she wouldn't have the same giddy physical response if, say, Lois had sent her a message about Joji. Or even if she'd gotten a text from her mother.

Lucy stood there, phone in hand, trying to come up with a good response to Dev as a few of the people from the Holiday Adventure Club group traipsed through the room on their way to another exhibit.

Hey yourself, she finally typed, her lips poised in a half-smile. *I promise I won't stiff you on the $32.87, and I can also guarantee that I won't stay in Venice forever, although it is beautiful. I'm headed to St. Barts next month for St. Patrick's Day—any ideas on how to advertise that, since you were the idea wizard behind this trip?*

Let me think about it, Dev shot back immediately. *I might have some ideas for you.*

Was that it? Lucy waited, watching the text box, and then the tell-tale three dots popped up, indicating that Dev was typing again.

Maybe we can kick it around together at the outdoor concert on the 21st? I got two tickets, and rumor is that the Foo Fighters will be there.

Lucy's heart leapt into her throat. Was Dev actually asking her on a date while she was on another continent? Or was he really just thinking they might go check out the concert and talk about advertising ideas? After all, he'd never so much as hinted at going out with her in the year and a half she'd known him. Her mini-relationship and subsequent messy breakup with Charlie had elicited noncommittal sympathy of the generic sort, but even after that, Dev had made no moves to flirt openly or to show her that he was interested.

I could do that, she sent back. That didn't feel like enough, so Lucy followed up with one more line and then forced herself to drop her phone into her purse: *If Dave Grohl will be there, I'll be there*, she said, referring to the Foo Fighters frontman. She wasn't sure if she should have gone with something more flirty, but it was Dev, after all, and froth and sugar were not his style.

"You coming along, Lucy?" Marge called out in the open room, stopping the *tap, tap, tap* of her cane against the marble floor as she paused and waited for Lucy to join her and Mrs. Severson. "We never even got around to the story about the time I caught Diane kissing the principal of the middle school on a field trip with a bunch of kids."

"Oh, you did not see that, you old fool," Mrs. Severson shot back, walking ahead of her friend toward the doorway to the next room.

"Doesn't mean it didn't happen," Marge said as an aside, mostly to Lucy, but loudly enough that everyone else in the room heard it too.

"A GONDOLA WILL BE THE BEST WAY TO SEE THE CITY AND COVER THE most ground," Bree said with authority as she and Carmen boarded a boat after breakfast.

"And what if we're stuck on a boat and we see your guy wandering the streets above us, oblivious to the fact that you're desperately trying to find him?"

Carmen settled in next to Bree just as the gondolier pushed off, smiling broadly as he steered them down the canal. With a triumphant face, Bree reached into her oversized purse and took out a rolled up piece of legal-sized printer paper. On it, she'd written with block letters in Sharpie: DO YOU HAVE MY PENNY? PLEASE BRING IT TO THE HOTEL CHIARA!!! And then scattered randomly in the corners of the page, she'd written the word REWARD three different times.

"Ooooh, good thinking, girl," Carmen said, nodding as she read it. "But maybe you should have put your phone number on it so he could just call or text you and you could meet him. You know, rather than leaving it up to him to do the legwork. That's kind of asking a lot."

"I don't think holding up a sign with my phone number on it for all of Venice to see is a wise move." Bree rolled the paper back up but kept it in her hand as she scooted around and got comfortable on the gondola. "Now, keep your eyes open. He could be anywhere."

As they glided beneath the bridges, they watched the streets and buildings, looking for the mysterious man with the penny.

"So," Bree said after fifteen minutes of intense face-searching masked as pleasant sightseeing, "are you gonna fill me in on why you got up on the wrong side of the bed today?"

Carmen shrugged. "I didn't," she said defensively. "I just felt tired. You know when you hit that point in a vacation where you kind of just want your own bed and your own house, but then you get mad at yourself for feeling that way because you're like, 'What is wrong with me? I am on *vacation* and I'm acting like I'm having a pap smear with a cold speculum or something.'"

Bree nodded. "Yes, I definitely know the feeling of wanting to wake up in your old life," she said quietly, watching the foot traffic overhead as they slipped beneath yet another bridge. Their gondolier waved at a man steering a boat nearby.

"God, Bree," Carmen said, setting one hand on Bree's white denim clad thigh. "I'm sorry. Of course you know that feeling. See? I just woke up with my head stuffed up my bum, and I'm making things about me, which is definitely not what I meant to do."

"Hey, I'm not the only one who's allowed to have feelings here." Bree gave a sad smile. "Just because I feel like I'm walking around the world wearing someone else's skin, or, like, seeing everything for the first time after having Lasik surgery, that doesn't mean you can't be homesick or hungry—or horny," she said, laughing a little at the last one.

"You know me too well, girl," Carmen said, reaching for the rolled up paper in Bree's hand. "I'm all three of those things at the moment, but mostly the last two."

"Well, I can definitely help you with the hungry part when lunchtime rolls around, but you're on your own to scratch that last itch."

"Deal." Carmen winked at her and then unrolled the paper one more time. "Good thinking on this, by the way." She winked at Bree with admiration. "I bet you were up early and down at the front desk of the hotel making this, weren't you?"

"Middle of the night," Bree admitted, tucking her straightened hair behind both ears shyly. "I woke up and thought of it, and figured I might as well get it done."

"You spend more time roaming that hotel in the middle of the night than you spend sleeping in it."

"Once I get my penny back I'll sleep like a baby. Promise."

"You know," Carmen said with a frown. "That saying always gets me because, not that either one of us know from firsthand experience, but don't babies wake up crying all night long? So why do we say 'sleep like a baby'?"

Bree considered this. "I think it's because they haven't been alive long enough to toss and turn from the anxiety of living on earth and adulting. You know? Other than waking up from a deep slumber wondering where their next boob is coming from, they don't really have any problems."

"So then why don't we say 'sleeping like a man'?" Carmen pulled a tube of lipstick and a pocket-sized mirror from her purse and started to fix her lips. "They wake up in the middle of the night wondering where their next boob is coming from, too."

"Because then we'd sound like sexist jerks."

"Fair." Carmen ran the creamy lipstick over her full lips before puckering them in the small mirror and snapping the compact shut. "Hey," she said, putting everything back into her purse and turning to Bree with a serious look. "Have you given any thought to what you're going to wish for when you get your penny back? Or did you already have the wish in your head?"

Bree was watching a woman above them on the street who was dressed in a tangerine orange column of sequins. She stood still as a statue behind her Carnival mask and wore a sleek orange wig cut into a bob.

As they passed, Bree tore her attention away from the woman in orange and looked at Carmen. "I'm not sure," she admitted. "I was about to wish something when the guy bumped me on the bridge, but now I couldn't tell you exactly what it was."

Carmen looked puzzled. "Don't you think you should have something concrete? I mean, given how important this is to you?"

"I'm kind of blocked, to be perfectly honest. I want to make the wish and toss the penny and make good on my promise, but I'm not entirely sure what to wish for. I can't wish for Kenny to come back, because duh. Also I'm not a ten-year-old girl who believes in magic."

Bree picked at her cuticles as she thought. "But I don't think it feels fair to just wish for my own happiness."

Carmen watched her friend intently. "Don't you think that's what Kenny would want you to wish for?"

Without hesitation, Bree nodded. "It is. Absolutely."

They rode along in amiable silence for a few minutes as they took in more Carnival-goers wandering around in broad daylight looking like extras from the set of Tom Cruise and Nicole Kidman's *Eyes Wide Shut*. But as soon as they emerged from beneath another bridge, Carmen grabbed Bree's arm with one hand and pointed with the other at the balcony of a building above them.

"Bree!" she shouted. "Is that him? Oh my god!" Carmen stood up, sending the gondola into a dangerous back-and-forth rocking motion.

"Sit! Please!" the gondolier shouted, lifting his paddle from the water and holding up a hand in warning.

Bree's eyes followed Carmen's finger and landed on a table situated right at the edge of a balcony that overlooked the canal. Sure enough, it was him. His dark curls were particularly loose and floppy that day, and instead of a navy blue sweater, he wore a camel-colored blazer over a t-shirt. His skin was warm and tanned and his attention had been drawn down to the water by the commotion. Bree rocketed to her feet, fumbling her rolled up paper as she did.

"Oh my god! Carmen! You found him!" she said, trying with shaking hands to unroll the message she'd written in the middle of the night.

"Here, I'll do it." Carmen reached for the paper at the same time that Bree was starting to unfurl it, but instead of each of them taking a side of the sign to hold up, they knocked hands and sent the paper flying over the side of the boat.

"No!" Bree called, scrambling for the rolled-up paper as the boat continued its perilous tipping motion. "Oh, no!" She looked up at the man, barely clocking his table companions as she tried to think of what to say. What to shout. How to get the message to him now that the paper was floating like soggy seaweed on the green water of the canal.

"Uh oh," Carmen said from behind her. "This isn't—"

But she didn't have time to finish the sentence before the boat gave one final, exaggerated tip, launching them both over the side and into the water.

"Oh, ladies," the gondolier said, looking down at them with disappointment as they flailed in the canal, drenched and spitting out water. Somehow, he'd managed to ride out the disaster and remain standing, holding his oar for balance.

Bree started to tread water as she reached for the note, catching the sodden paper in one hand and holding it up pointlessly. As she held it, the paper ripped in half from the weight of the water and she let it go, opting to stay afloat instead by using both arms to paddle.

"Good thing you flat-ironed your hair," Carmen said, trying not to laugh as she looked at Bree in her soaking wet red turtleneck sweater and stringy, water-logged hair.

"Good thing you just fixed your makeup," Bree retorted. A laugh was starting to bubble up inside of her despite the circumstances.

"Hey, are you okay?" a man in a black jacket shouted as he leaned over the balcony, hanging onto the railing and looking at them with concern. Bree realized that he was one of the men who'd been eating with the penny thief.

"We're okay!" Carmen called back, her words echoing off the buildings that ran along the canal.

The man with the dark curls came and stood next to his friend for a moment, watching them with amusement. "Well, what do you know? This canal looks like American soup!" he shouted in an Australian accent, laughing uproariously at his own joke. He turned to his friend and whacked him on the arm. "Get it? American soup?" When he looked back at Bree and Carmen, he cupped his mouth with both hands theatrically. "Hang on, I'll come save you!"

"Oh my god, he's coming down here," Bree said, treading water more furiously than before.

They looked back up just in time to see the man in the black coat pull a wallet from inside the breast pocket of his jacket. He opened it, grabbed a handful of bills, and dropped them on the table.

"Yes, Joseph will be right down to save you," the man shouted with an amused smirk. "Keep swimming, ladies."

Carmen and Bree looked up at him with wide eyes. "Joseph," Carmen said, splashing the water and spraying Bree to get her attention. "His name is Joseph and he's coming to fish us out of the canal."

But in the meantime, the gondolier tossed them both life preservers, which the women grabbed with gratitude as they waited for Joseph to emerge from the building.

Carmen was smoothing her wet curls with one hand and hanging onto the flotation device with the other when a little speedboat with two uniformed water rescuers on it came zipping across the water, kicking up waves with its motor.

"Here you are," one of the rescuers said in thickly-accented English, holding out a hand to Bree. "Let me pull you."

"But—" Bree wanted to wait for Joseph to come and save her so that she could latch onto him and not let go until he gave her back that penny. "I can't." She felt like yanking her hand free of the rescuer's and swimming in the other direction, but she knew that would be a crazy thing to do.

In the end it didn't matter because, mistaking her words for a warning that she was too weak to help lift herself, the rescuer grabbed both of Bree's arms firmly and pulled her onto the boat. Next, they fished Carmen out of the canal and plopped her down on the bench seat next to Bree, where they offered both women insulated blankets to wrap around themselves as they sped toward dry land.

Bree protested loudly and in words that she hoped the Italian rescuers might understand, but before she could stop them, they'd revved up the boat's motor and were racing across the water, her words drowned out by the loud *whir* of the motor.

Bree turned around as they sped away, keeping her eyes on the street that overlooked the canal. They were completely out of earshot when the men finally emerged from the building, one in a black jacket, the other in a camel-colored coat and, oddly, a pair of sweat pants tucked into UGG boots. They watched with their hands on their hips as the boat disappeared.

Fruitlessly and without any real energy behind it, Bree's lips formed the word as her hand raised in farewell: "Joseph."

11

FEBRUARY 13
VENICE, ITALY

Lucy was dressed for cocktail hour in an off-the-shoulder yellow dress that showed off her year-round Florida tan. Her hair was swept back, and from her ears dangled two long, colorful strings of beads. Her orange clutch purse was tucked under one arm, and the other hand was poised on the doorknob to her hotel room when a loud knock on the other side of the door startled her.

She looked out the peephole. *Bree.* Without hesitation, Lucy opened the door.

"Hey!" Her wide smile faded as she took in Bree's now dry but still stringy hair, the pools of mascara under her eyes, and the frantic look on her face. "What's wrong?" Lucy took a step back, clocking the situation with a sweeping head-to-toe glance. "Are you okay?"

Bree leaned on the doorframe with one shoulder and ran a hand through her tangled hair. "I fell into the canal."

"We both did!" Carmen shouted from down the hotel hallway. Somehow, her wet hair had just sprung back into its usual curly state and she'd already taken the time to wipe off the remnants of that morning's makeup. "We were in the gondola," she started to explain as she reached Lucy's door.

"And we saw him—the guy—on a balcony having lunch," Bree cut in.

"So we both stood up and accidentally rocked the boat because Bree had this sign she wanted to hold up—"

"—with the name of the hotel so he could bring the penny here!"

"But then we fell into the canal," Carmen finished, casting a sideways glance at Bree's messy hair and face as if to remind herself of the boat tragedy and its outcome. "And his friend said his name."

"Which is Joseph," Bree said, still sounding breathless and like she'd just run up eight flights of stairs to get to Lucy's room. "His name is Joseph, and he wears sweatpants with UGGs and I think he's Australian."

Lucy stood there, listening to this exchange as she tried to push away the sound of Honey's voice in her head, telling her over her pedicure just days earlier that someone would fall into a canal in Venice on this trip. All at once, she remembered the other part of Honey's prophecy: that she'd help someone get back something they'd lost. She'd had no idea at the time what that item might be, or even whether it was tangible, but now she knew that it was the penny. *The penny! Of course!* And that was only if she were laboring under the assumption that it was even possible for Honey to predict the future or to know in advance the events that might happen. With enough years of science under her belt, Lucy found that it was sometimes nearly impossible to suspend her disbelief, but to her own surprise, she found that she wanted to. She really wanted to.

"Come in." Lucy opened her door wider and waved the women into the sitting area.

"But you were on your way out," Bree said with dismay, looking at Lucy's outfit. "And you look so cute! I don't want to keep you."

"It's okay," Lucy assured them, setting her purse on the coffee table in front of the couch. "It's just cocktail hour in the lobby for the Holiday Adventure Club group. No biggie. These are all adults who are fully capable of having a drink and an hors d'oeuvre without my guidance." She opened the minibar and pulled out a couple of small bottles of water, handing one to each of the women as they sat on her couch. "So what happened? Did you get the penny?"

Bree twisted open the cap to her water bottle and took a big swig. "No! Some boat rescue thing—like the Italian Coast Guard—came along right away and dragged us out of the water and whisked us away."

"But not before Joseph yelled down from the balcony that we'd turned the canal into American soup," Carmen added, laughing.

"Witty," Lucy said. "And he's as cute as the video?"

"Cuter," Carmen said, nodding.

"Stop," Bree said. "He's not *ugly*, but he's just the guy who has my penny. That's all. And," she said, looking slightly amused, "he has kind of weird fashion sense."

"He's the cute, funny guy who has your penny," Carmen clarified. "And he has a sexy Australian accent. And...okay, let's call his fashion choices *unique*."

"Australian, huh?" Lucy's eyebrows shot up.

"Yep," Carmen said with a smirk. "I've had some good times with Australian men, so I'm on Team Joseph here, and I'd even let him keep the UGGs on."

"Ooooh." Lucy bit on her bottom lip. "Sounds—" She'd almost said "sounds hot," but then stopped herself because should she really be *oohing* and *ahhing* over some hot Australian guy when Bree was only hunting him down to retrieve the penny that belonged to her late husband? Probably not. Lucy cleared her throat and attempted to harness the sense of gravity she'd always worn like a cloak when dealing with the bereaved in her old job. "It sounds like a problem," she said instead, nodding and trying to look noncommittal.

"It is," Bree went on, her eyes filling with frustrated tears. "Because we lost him again and we're now spending all our time in Venice chasing after some guy, which kind of pisses me off. There are plenty of other exciting things we could be doing here besides this."

"Hey," Carmen said, reaching over to grab Bree's hand. She held it tightly and squeezed to get Bree's attention. "Who cares? I'm having a great time and this is an adventure. I promise you, we'll never forget this trip."

"Yeah?" Bree smiled through her tears, wiping under her eyes with the hand that wasn't clutched in Carmen's.

"Yeah," Carmen reassured her gently. "And we're gonna find old Joey—mark my words."

Lucy grabbed her purse from the table and pulled out her phone. "You know," she said, watching as the screen came to life. "We can do better than holding up signs and swimming in canals to find this guy —no offense," she added, looking up at Bree's face. "The sign was a great idea. But listen, we're three smart Millennial women who are thinking like Boomers."

Carmen snorted.

"I'm serious," Lucy said. "I'm not just throwing shade at Boomers, but their use of technology is different than ours. My friend Dev is the one who helped me finally figure out how to advertise this trip, and he had some really good ideas that revolved around social media." Lucy felt a tiny thrill that started in her toes at the mention of Dev's name, but she tried to ignore it as she tapped open the app for Twitter. "So I want us to put on our thinking caps and harness the power of the internet right now, got it?"

"I'm game," Bree said, twisting her limp hair into a bun at the nape of her neck and tying it off haphazardly with an elastic she'd been wearing on her left wrist. "Let's do this."

"First, we're gonna post that still shot from the video," Lucy said, opening up a blank tweet on her phone. She didn't have a personal Twitter account, so this would have to come from her Holiday Adventure Club profile. In short order, she set up the tweet, attached the photo, and then handed her phone over to Bree and Carmen, seated side by side on the couch, so that they could huddle over it and approve her post.

Help!!! A wish was made at the Bridge of Sighs, the penny was mistakenly stolen, and now we're trying to catch this guy before he runs off with someone else's good luck! Last seen: Venice, Italy. Description: cute, curly-

haired, funny. Sounds Australian. Answers to: Joseph. Do you know this man? All leads welcome. #venice #lost #pleasereturn #hotguy

"I'm not sure if the 'hot guy' hashtag is necessary," Bree said, handing the phone back. "But otherwise I'm on board."

"I mean...facts are facts," Carmen said, shrugging. "I say leave the 'hot guys' in there and get more eyes on this tweet."

"So we're good?" Lucy looked up at them both with her thumb poised over the "tweet" button.

"Go for it." Bree nodded firmly.

"Okay, done. Now, I think we post in some Facebook groups—maybe find some that are dedicated to Venice, Carnival, stuff like that. And then use Instagram as well." Lucy waved a hand in the air dismissively. "I don't need to explain this. You both know how things go viral. We just need the right person to pick it up and spread it around."

"Honestly, it can't hurt," Carmen said, eyebrows lifted as she shook her head. "Our only other plan was to race around Venice searching through crowds of thousands of masked strangers to find him."

"Seriously," Bree said, turning both palms to the ceiling. "How did I not think of something better than holding up a sign? You're right, Lucy. I'm not thinking straight. I deserve to get my cool card revoked immediately."

Carmen gave Bree a once over. "Sweetie, if you keep walking around looking like that, no one is ever going to believe that you once *had* a cool card to revoke in the first place."

"So you're saying I should shower?" Bree looked down at the sweatpants and long-sleeved t-shirt she'd thrown on the minute they'd gotten back to the hotel and stripped off their wet canal clothes.

"I think you should *both* get ready and come to happy hour in the lobby," Lucy said, standing up and slipping her phone back into her purse. "I've got dinner reservations at Il Formaggio tonight and I'd love for you guys to come with me."

Carmen stood and offered a hand to Bree, pulling her to her feet.

"We'll be there. Give us like thirty minutes to freshen up," she paused and appraised Bree with a skeptical look. "Or maybe forty-five."

"Ha. Do I look that bad?" Bree blinked a few times and felt the gritty leftover mascara coating her eyes. "God, I do, don't I?"

"You just need a little work, girl," Carmen said gently. Then, to Lucy: "We'll be in the lobby in an hour."

Lucy walked them to the door and waited as they ambled down the hall, giving them a last wave as they disappeared into the elevator. As much as she'd expected to come on this trip and just handle the menial details of her travelers' days, she realized that she was actually having *fun*. It'd been a while since she'd had girlfriends who weren't either colleagues or people she'd met in the medical program in college, and she was completely drawn to Carmen and Bree. Their friendship with one another was obviously genuine and deep, and it was easy for Lucy to sympathize with Bree's situation and to root for her as she found her way as a widow.

As an adult, it had been somewhat of a challenge for Lucy to balance the kind of fun, let's-meet-for-cocktails type of female friendships she craved with the intensity of her career or with the level of attention that her mom required, and even when she'd first moved to Amelia Island and lived with Katrina, she'd never really let her guard down and considered her to be more than a roommate. And thank god for that, or she would have lost more than a boyfriend and a girl she simply shared an apartment with when Charlie and Katrina got together. As it was, the loss of the two of them was truly no great loss at all. It had been a blow to her self-esteem, sure, but nothing more.

But this—this was fun. This was what it felt like to share confidences and kick around ideas and have dinner plans with other women, and Lucy loved it. More importantly, she needed it.

As the elevator closed behind them, Lucy ducked back into her room to grab a sweater for the chilly night ahead.

By the time the women had finished their mojitos in the lobby, there were already several hits on the social media posts.

"Let's head over to the restaurant and read what we got," Lucy said. "Just let me check in with everyone to make sure they're good for the evening here."

Carmen and Bree watched as Lucy made the rounds, stopping to chat with Marge and Mrs. Severson to check that they were all set up for dinner and had evening plans. Marge tapped the toe of Lucy's shoe with her sparkly cane. She said something that looked like she was barking orders at the younger woman. Carmen gave a little huff of a laugh as she watched this exchange take place.

"You know, she might have taken offense when I said she would make a good cruise director, but I'm not joking. Just look at her." Carmen tipped her head at Lucy as she fielded a question from creepy New Jersey Richard and his long-suffering wife. "Ugh, remember that guy?" She made a face at Richard.

"He's a handful," Bree agreed, setting her empty mojito glass on a tray with a collection of other glasses that held only half-melted ice cubes and sprigs of damp mint. "I don't envy his wife one bit."

"She's probably crazy in love with him," Carmen said as her eyes roved Richard's protruding stomach, receding hairline, and gold pinky rings on both hands. "A perfect example of the many ways that love is blind."

"It would have to be, or we'd all die alone, single till the end," Bree added.

"Oh stop. You found someone to marry you once—it could happen again. That gives all of us hope, you know? And I do think it's worth mentioning here that I myself haven't yet been able to rope anyone into showing up at the altar."

Bree exhaled loudly through her nostrils in response. Carmen could have *easily* gone the marriage and family route had she wanted to, but as far as Bree knew, she'd never desired that. Instead of taking the bait from Carmen, she focused her eyes on Lucy, admiring how pretty she looked in her yellow dress, cute ankle boots, and denim jacket. Her face lit up with a friendly smile as she talked to the other Holiday Adventure Clubbers.

"What about Lucy? Do you think she's married?" Carmen asked.

"She hasn't really said anything about her private life, now that you mention it. Here I am, going on and on about my problems and my life to her in a bar in the middle of the night on the day we arrived in Venice, and I never even bothered to ask if she was married or had kids."

"I think you can be forgiven," Carmen said. "People can get so touchy when you ask about things like that. Sometimes it's just that they've never settled down even though they really wanted to, or maybe kids haven't come along as easily as they'd hoped. So I think it's okay not to ask that kind of personal stuff right out of the gate."

"True." Bree chewed on the side of her thumbnail for a second as she watched Lucy laugh and touch someone's arm warmly. "But I hope she has someone. She's one of those girls who clearly doesn't see herself as she really is. Do you know what I'm saying?"

"I know exactly what you're saying," Carmen said pointedly. "Like a cool girl who has no idea that she's actually a cool girl."

"Oh my god, I am *not* cool," Bree said when she picked up on Carmen's meaning. She shifted her purse from one shoulder to the other. "I'm just a boring widow from Portland who works all day, and watches documentaries all evening."

"Whoa." Carmen blinked a few times. "It never stops giving me a weird little shock when I hear you call yourself a widow. That word always makes me think of an eighty-year-old woman who wears black all the time and talks to a picture of her dead husband."

Bree's cheeks went pink.

"Oh god—I am so, so sorry, Bree. If you talk to Kenny's picture then I am totally *not* making fun of that. I swear." Carmen pressed both of her hands to her chest as she watched her friend's face to see whether she'd offended her.

"Come on," Bree said. "I don't think you're making fun of me. And I definitely catch myself talking to him sometimes. How could I not? I spoke to the man every day for eight years of my life, and then one day I woke up and he was gone. So yeah, I still run things by him. He doesn't always answer, but I still talk to him like he's there."

"I hear you," Carmen said, squeezing Bree's hand in hers. "Hey, Lucy is done talking to people. How about we snag her and go track down some pasta? I'm starving."

"Me too. And I'm dying to know who's responded to the tweet about Joseph."

"Are we ready, girls?" Lucy asked Carmen and Bree, smiling as they approached her. She waved at a couple from their group who were holding hands as they walked across the lobby with their Carnival masks in hand.

"For pasta and wine?" Carmen looped her arm through Bree's. "Always."

The women talked and laughed as they walked through the darkness of early evening, pointing out the best costumes and stopping to snap pictures as they strolled. A man dressed as a harlequin was bent down on one knee before a woman who was made up like the Queen of Hearts. He handed her half a dozen red roses with overplayed, dramatic hand gestures as the crowd looked on, amused by the silent show of romance they were putting on.

Il Formaggio was situated at one end of a footbridge. Its patio was covered with cozy tables and warmed by several tall propane heaters that were scattered amongst the diners. The hostess showed them to a table for four that was nestled at the edge of the outdoor seating area with a great view of everyone who passed by. As they watched, costumed tourists walked by, talking excitedly and shooting video and pictures of themselves and of the boats on the canal.

"Should we start with a bottle of red and a run-through of our new Twitter friends who are going to help us find Joseph?" Carmen asked, eyes flicking over a menu on the table.

"Sounds good to me." Lucy pulled her phone out of her purse and opened Twitter. "Looks like we have...oh, God. We've already gotten over a hundred replies!"

"What?" Bree leaned forward in her chair, craning her neck to try and read Lucy's phone screen. "Sorry," she said. "I didn't mean to jump into your personal space like that." Bree scooted back and held up both hands when she realized that she'd basically vaulted into Lucy's lap.

Without even looking up from her phone, Lucy made a dismissive sound and waved a hand. "Don't even worry about it. In fact, bring your chair around next to me so we can both read these."

Carmen flagged down an incredibly good looking waiter with smoldering eyes and knife-sharp cheekbones and when he was finally standing next to their table, she looked up at him coquettishly and ordered wine and an appetizer of ricotta and pancetta bruschetta while Bree scooted her chair closer to Lucy. Together, they scrolled through messages that were mostly just encouragement or people tagging friends and commenting on how cool Carnival was, but every so often someone offered a tidbit or a suggestion.

"*Hey, my brother is there right now,*" Lucy read aloud. "*I'm tagging him so he can help you if you need it!*"

"*That hot guy you posted kind of looks like my college roommate's Italian fling from a week we spent in Sicily in 2014,*" Bree read. "*But I feel like his name was Antonio or Roberto or something...*" She stopped reading and put her hands over her eyes, breathing in and out deeply as the waiter returned to pour three glasses of wine. He waited patiently for each of the women to taste it and approve the bottle.

"Delicious," Lucy said, taking another sip.

Bree lifted her glass to indicate that she was pleased with the wine.

"*Grazie,*" Carmen said to him, adding a completely unnecessary wink and a glance at his retreating backside. When Bree caught her ogling the waiter, Carmen gave a tiny, helpless shrug paired with a look of pure innocence, as if to say *So? It was worth a look.*

"How about this one?" Lucy offered, completely unaware of the entire exchange between Bree and Carmen that had just gone on at their table. She took another small sip of her wine and then read aloud: "*I'm pretty sure that's Joseph Mancini. The pic is a little blurry, but it looks like him. @JoeManItaly is this you???*"

The three women made eye contact over the candle flickering on the table. Carmen let out a low whistle. "That actually sounds kind of promising."

"Any responses yet?" Bree chewed on the side of her thumbnail again, a habit she'd picked up during the long months of Kenny's declining health. It was something she'd stopped doing recently, but the search for the missing penny had rekindled a low-grade anxiousness inside of her, and she'd gone back to nibbling her finger without even realizing she was doing it.

Lucy refreshed Twitter and waited. "Nothing yet. But I have an idea." Her thumbs began to fly over the keyboard as she tapped something out on the screen. "How about this?" Lucy cleared her throat and read: "*Hey @JoeManItaly, if this is you and you're in Venice at the moment, come to Il Formaggio and meet us. We're sitting outside on the patio right now.*" She snapped a quick photo of Bree and Carmen with wineglasses in hand as they talked and attached it to the tweet.

Bree sucked in a sharp breath, imagining Joseph strolling over the footbridge and approaching their table. Her heart raced inexplicably for a moment as she pictured how that conversation would unfold.

Carmen leveled a gaze at Bree as understanding passed between them. "This does seem like the fastest way to either get him to reply to the tweet, or to get him to show up here with your penny." She lifted her wine glass to her lips. "But you make the final call, girl."

Without hesitation, Bree nodded. "Yeah," she said. "Yes. Do it."

Lucy posted the tweet and locked her phone. "Okay. Now let's order dinner and see what happens, huh?"

They picked up menus and tried to busy themselves with choosing pasta and salads, pretending that they weren't all cutting their eyes to the footbridge or looking the other direction every thirty seconds.

"Hey, girls," Carmen said, leaning back as the waiter set a plate of fettuccini in front of her and then used a giant grinder to sprinkle it with freshly ground black pepper. "We can do better than this. We're three women out for dinner in Venice, and we're anxiously hoping some fairly hot random dude will show up here with a penny. Let's just put him out of our minds for a while, okay?"

Bree twirled her spaghetti around a fork and nodded. "Definitely. He's not really the focus of this whole mission anyway. The penny is. I don't care at all that he's cute."

Lucy and Carmen exchanged the most fleeting, almost non-existent look that two women ever exchanged, and yet it was there. They looked back at their plates of pasta simultaneously, trying to pretend that they both hadn't—at the very same moment—hoped just briefly that Bree might meet a nice guy who would help her take the first step into the rest of her life.

"So Lucy," Carmen said, lifting a forkful of fettuccini. "Tell us more about you."

Lucy chewed and swallowed a bite of mozzarella and tomato from her *caprese* salad. "About me?" She took a swig of her sparkling water and then set her fork on the plate. "Okay," Lucy said, wiping her hands on the napkin in her lap. "Well, I'm single. Divorced, no kids. I grew up in Buffalo and moved to Florida about a year and a half ago. I started The Holiday Adventure Club travel agency as a way to kind of reinvent myself and my life and it's been a little challenging," she admitted. "There are still plenty of people who want to hire someone to plan everything for them when it comes to travel, but I had to work hard to find my niche, you know?"

Carmen held her curly hair away from her face with one hand as she leaned over her plate and took a huge bite of fettuccini. "Were you in the travel industry in Buffalo?"

"Actually, no." Lucy set her fork on the edge of her plate and leaned back in her chair. "I was a forensic pathologist."

Bree choked on her pasta. "You mean, you did autopsies? You're a doctor?"

Lucy nodded. "Yes and yes. And I needed a change, so I left."

"Wow." Carmen had stopped eating and was watching Lucy. "That's not just a small change like selling car insurance for ten years and then switching to life insurance. And Buffalo to Florida—also not a small change."

Lucy shrugged and picked up her fork so that she could push her salad around. "Things were really stagnating for me," she admitted, looking back and forth between Carmen and Bree. Talking about her life out loud felt foreign, but also good. "As I said, I was married, but my husband decided he wanted to be with someone younger. Someone more fun." She shrugged like it didn't matter, but the move wasn't careless at all. Her eyes went back to her plate and fixated on the cherry red tomatoes there as she pressed the tines of her fork against them, releasing their juices like a trickle of blood. "So that happened. And I'm the primary caregiver—or I was—for my mother, who is agoraphobic and was just recently diagnosed with dementia. The combination of those two things, the bleak weather, and the amount of dead bodies I saw in any given week just kind of got to me. I hit a wall and I left for my own mental health."

Carmen and Bree were openly staring at Lucy's face.

"God," Bree said, shaking her head. "That's a lot for anyone to handle. Any one of those things would be enough to push someone over the edge."

Carmen squinted at Lucy across the table. "I think it took balls to leave all that behind and do something new."

Lucy's lips twitched and she looked at Carmen directly. "Thank you. Sometimes it feels insane. and I had a bit of a rough start when I got to Amelia Island, so there were real moments of me second-guessing myself."

"What happened?" Bree put a forkful of pasta to her mouth and chewed, though Lucy could tell that she wasn't even paying attention to her food at that point.

"I wanted to buy a little house, but I felt like it was best to rent for the first six months and get the lay of the land so I could make a more informed decision. I moved in with this random girl and came home one day to find her in bed with the guy I'd just started dating. It threw me for a bit of a loop."

Carmen gave her an incredulous look. "Oh *hell* no," she said, shaking her head indignantly. "That's not how girl code works." She had a knife in one hand, a fork in the other and a vicious gleam in her eyes. If Katrina had been there at the table as Lucy told the story, she felt pretty sure that things wouldn't have ended well for her ex-roommate.

"It was fine," Lucy said. It made her tired to even think of Charlie and Katrina. "We weren't great friends anyway and the guy wasn't even that good in bed, so she can keep him."

Bree and Carmen hooted appreciatively. "Damn, girl!" Carmen said, shaking her head as she speared another bite of pasta. "Okay." Carmen leveled her gaze on Lucy. "Let's talk love—not that guy you caught red-handed with whatserface, and not the ex either; we don't care about them at the moment. You got anyone on your island you're currently into?"

Lucy's cheeks flamed. "Actually, there are two guys," she said, the words spilling out before she could stop them. "My office is sandwiched between the businesses of the two hottest guys on Amelia Island."

Carmen grabbed the wine bottle and topped up all three glasses. "Okay, girl. I see you, I see you," she said with a look of deep admiration. She set the bottle on the table. "Game recognizes game. Go on."

"Well, Nick runs the postal store on one side of me," Lucy said, swirling her wine around in her glass as she conjured an image of a shirtless Nick on the phone. "He's got a cute dog and loves books, and he's the kind of guy you feel safe with. I feel like I'm always smiling when I'm with him."

"I like the way he sounds," Bree said, nodding and tearing a hunk of bread to dip in the olive oil that the waiter had brought to their table. "But I can admit that I'm partial to a guy who reads."

"And then there's Dev." Lucy's eyes darkened as she thought of his strong arms and the way he took everything so seriously. "He owns the coffee shop on the other side of the travel agency. He's one of those prototypical 'tall, dark, handsome, and mysterious' types."

"Ooooh, so far so good." Carmen lifted her wine glass and tipped it in Lucy's direction. "Either one of these delicious men might erase the bad memories you got from those other dudes."

"Honestly," Lucy agreed. "When I'm with Dev, I feel..." She squinted, trying to put the feeling into words. "Like anything could happen. He's not really dangerous, per se, but he is sort of wild and untamed."

"Motorcycle?" There was a knowing look in Carmen's eyes.

"Yep."

"I've had a few Devs in my life." Carmen pursed her lips and set her wine glass on the table. "Fun. Sexy. Makes your heart race but always leaves you wanting more."

Lucy leaned back in her chair and ran her napkin between her fingers. "He asked me to go to a concert when I get back."

"That sounds promising." Carmen lifted an eyebrow. "But it really depends on what concert. This is going to be very telling—is he taking you to a country jamboree? Or is it death metal? I'm gonna need more info before I make a final judgment."

"Foo Fighters," Lucy said. "Actually, he told me they were scheduled to be there. Could be other bands as well."

"Alright. So he's a cool cat." Carmen nodded and tucked into her pasta again, but kept her eyes on Lucy's face. "And if you go to this concert with Mr. Hot and Possibly Dangerous, what will Mr. Book-in-his-back-pocket say about it?"

Lucy swallowed hard and stalled. "I feel like he might not like it. He never says a word about Dev," she added in a rush. "But sometimes I feel a tiny bit of friction when I mention one of them to the other. Which I don't do on purpose!" she blurted as a quick addendum. "I would never play one guy off of another on purpose."

Carmen looked deeply amused. "And why not?"

Lucy considered the question. "Because. That's not nice."

"Is love always nice?" Carmen challenged.

"I think it *should* be," Bree said, adding her two cents. "In a perfect world."

"Well, there is no such thing as a perfect world," Carmen said resolutely. "There is an *im*perfect world filled with *im*perfect people, and we do our best to navigate it all without hurting ourselves or each other. Does that mean we're always successful?" She waved her fork around as she talked, eyes roving the faces at the tables around them.

"No. We're not. But I would imagine that both of your hot island men have enough life experience under their belts to know that. So I would worry less about how you're handling things with them, and more about figuring out which of them—if either—makes you truly happy."

"That's fair," Bree said. "I've got to agree with that. At a certain age, we understand that life and love are complicated."

Lucy was about to speak up when she spotted a tall, cute guy with dark curls approaching Il Formaggio with a single red rose in his hand and a look of anticipation on his face.

"Damn," Lucy said. Her fork dropped and clattered against her pasta dish. "Is that him? Is that our guy from Twitter?"

Bree nearly gave herself whiplash as she spun to look. "Oh god," she whispered. "That *is* him."

Carmen leaned sideways so that she could take him in as he strode purposefully toward the restaurant's patio area. "Yep," she said with a smirk, tipping her head to watch him. "That's our boy. And he's wearing a giant puffy jacket that looks like it's made out of an Australian flag."

Bree took a deep breath and stood, letting her forgotten napkin fall to the ground from her lap as she tried to steady herself with one hand against the edge of the table. She gave a half-hearted wave, but didn't smile.

With a somewhat sheepish grin, Joseph approached the table. "Hi," he said, dipping his chin and looking at the three women through a fringe of dark, thick eyelashes. "Excuse me for interrupting your dinner, ladies."

His coat was truly an exceptionally loud item of clothing. Bree frowned at it for a second before looking into his eyes.

"As long as you've got the penny, then no apology needed. And really, we should be thanking *you* for reading the tweet and coming all the way over here," Bree said, trying to squash the nervous feeling that was rushing through her body.

Joseph thrust the red rose at Bree. "I got this for you. I figured since I took your penny and possibly interrupted whatever wish you were making, I could at least bring you something beautiful to set things right."

Bree took the flower. She put the bud to her nose instinctively and breathed in the sweet smell of the rose. "Thank you, but that was totally unnecessary," she said, setting the rose gently beside her plate. "I just really need to get that penny."

Joseph slipped both hands into the pockets of his black pants and looked at Bree through his lashes again. "There's a slight situation with the penny," he said. "Very small detail."

Bree's face drained of color as she stared at him. This felt a little like the time she'd been told that Kenny was a young, healthy man, *except* that he had a fatal disease. "What. What do you mean? What are you saying? Did you lose it?"

"No, no. Nothing like that." Joseph held up both of his hands to fend off the horrified look that was creeping across Bree's face. "I just thought maybe we could make a bargain."

"A *bargain*?" Bree let the flower fall to her side. "Are you holding my penny hostage? Is that it? Are you asking me to pay you for it?"

Joseph looked around uncomfortably. The other diners were staring. "Of course not," he said, looking mildly offended as he lowered his voice. "I'm not looking for money. I just wanted to get to know you."

"But..." Bree looked back and forth between Carmen and Lucy wildly. This was uncharted territory, and she hadn't been prepared for anything other than finding this man and getting her penny back quickly and easily. "But, no," she finally said. "I need it now."

Something flickered behind Joseph's eyes. "You need it? Now?" he asked, giving her a playful look. He was clearly unaware that teasing Bree was the absolute wrong move to make.

"Yes!" she shouted, this time not caring who heard or how many people stared at them and listened in on this ridiculous discussion. "I need it and you'd better hand it over." Bree thrust out a hand, palm turned up, ready to accept her penny. She realized as the words came out of her mouth that she sounded like a middle schooler demanding that the bus bully hand over her book bag and stop taunting her with it.

Joseph chuckled. "Okay, I'll hand it over," he said, shifting on his feet. "Just meet me tomorrow and I'll have it for you." He turned and started to walk away.

"No!" Bree said loudly, stepping around the table and into the cobblestone street. She clenched her fists at her sides as she waited for him to turn back. "I need it *now!*"

Joseph glanced back. "Tomorrow!" he called.

"But how do I even know where to meet you?" Bree stepped to the side as a large group of Carnival revelers approached, weaving their way around her and swallowing her small frame into their masked, glittering midst. "You never said where to meet!" she yelled as a man bumped into her shoulder.

Joseph turned around and walked backward for a few steps as he cupped his mouth, yelling to be heard over the crowd. "I'll tweet you!"

Bree couldn't be certain, but she was pretty sure that she saw a maddening, self-satisfied smile on Joseph's face as he turned around and disappeared into the throng of people in the street.

12

FEBRUARY 14
VENICE, ITALY

T he phone buzzed on the nightstand next to Bree and startled her out of a deep sleep. After the initial bout of sleeplessness when they'd arrived, she'd settled into the kind of sleep that only came from exhaustion. She pulled the pillow from her head and pushed her hair out of her eyes as she reached for it.

Squinting at the screen, she saw a message from Lucy: *You up? We got a tweet from @JoeManItaly.*

Bree sat up, clutching the blanket and sheets to her chest as she re-read the message. Why was this guy making things so difficult for her? Why couldn't he just hand over the damn penny and be on his merry way? Under different circumstances, Bree could imagine that this might feel like some kind of romantic scavenger hunt put on by a cute stranger, but the circumstances *weren't* different; she was still a widow with a wish to make, and until she did that, she'd never stop pouring herself a glass of wine after work and settling in on her couch with a cocoon of blankets and the remote. She'd never accept the offer of a drink with a coworker, never take a date to a wedding or a birthday party, and, God forbid, she'd never let Carmen set her up on a dating app. *Nope, nope, nope, never.*

She let out a huff of frustration and threw the bedding aside. The last thing she needed was to play games with infuriating Joseph in his puffy flag coat.

I'm up, Bree texted back. *What did he say?*

I'll forward his message. Here you go:

Bree waited a beat as Lucy's message came through. Finally, a screenshot from Joseph's Twitter feed appeared:

@HolidayAdventureClub Penny Girl! Today is a day for romance and chance, so it only seems right that we'll follow in the footsteps of Casanova. Meet me at the clock tower in St. Mark's Square at 11:00. We'll take a private tour of Casanova's Venice. Wear your Carnival mask!

Bree's fingers flew over the keyboard as she started to reply to Lucy about how ridiculous this request was, but she paused. After a second of consideration, she deleted her indignant message and started over.

Okay, she said. *I'll do it his way. And I guess I'll get a free tour of Venice out of it, which is great, because all I've done so far is run around searching for my penny.*

Lucy's message appeared almost instantly: *And you fell into a canal. Don't forget that part.*

A smile spread across Bree's face. *A simple girl from Portland comes to Venice and falls headfirst into a canal. Trust me—I won't EVER forget that!*

See you at breakfast before your Casanova tour? Lucy asked.

Oh, definitely. I'll need coffee. See you in a bit.

Bree set her phone back on the nightstand and pulled the covers over her body again. She stared at the ceiling and blinked a few times. Did meeting Joseph for this tour count as a date? Was she being forced against her will into going on her first date since Kenny died? Would he be okay with it? Was *she* okay with it?

Thoughts turned in her head like wooden horses on a carousel, spinning round and round as she considered this strange predicament from all angles. Sure, Kenny had been an orderly, by-the-book kind of guy, but losing him had taken away some of Bree's spontaneity and her willingness to step outside her own little box. In essence, it had made *her* more like *him*. And as much as she'd loved Kenny, she'd never really aspired to be *like* him, but rather to be herself—to complement his attributes with the things that made her unique.

Was she losing those things—those parts of herself that she actually liked? Would this current version of Breanne Wineland-Jones ever consider opening a food cart or taking a Latin dance class? She had to admit that she probably wouldn't. So should she show up for this Casanova tour not just to get her penny, but to sample some of the things that the world outside of her job and her little house in Portland had to offer? Deep down she knew that it was time to force herself to pack up a little of the careful, reserved Kenny-ness she'd recently adopted, and to unbox some of the fun and frivolousness that she'd wrapped in tissue paper and carefully stored away when he died.

Bree folded her arms over the top of the bed covers and sighed deeply. Change would be hard. Newness would be uncomfortable. Letting go would be gut-wrenching. But she knew in her heart that it was time.

"Carm?" she called out, hoping that her voice would rouse Carmen in the other room of their suite. "Wanna go to breakfast with me?"

"Mmmm," Carmen moaned from her own bedroom.

"I hope that means yes," Bree said, standing up and stretching her arms overhead. "Because I need to get ready. Apparently I have a date at eleven with The Penny Thief."

"Say what, girl?" Carmen's voice rang out loud and clear.

"You heard me. He tweeted at Lucy this morning and she already texted me. So get your butt out of bed and take me downstairs for coffee."

Carmen poked her head through the doorway; her hair was a tangle of curls and she had a pink satin sleep mask shoved up onto her forehead. "I'll be ready in ten."

WITH LUCY AND CARMEN'S EXCITED CHATTER AND ADVICE TO RELAX and just be herself still ringing in her ears, Bree approached the clock tower at St. Mark's Square just before eleven. The weather had taken a sharp turn from mild winter sun and unthreatening cloud cover, to temperatures hovering just above freezing. But Bree was a Pacific Northwest girl and therefore prepared for anything the sky wanted to throw at her, so she traipsed across Venice with her hands tucked into warm gloves, feet clad in thick socks and boots, and a pink wool coat buttoned around her.

She'd tried to tell the other women that while this smacked of a real date, it was honestly just a chance to get out and see Venice while achieving her ultimate goal: getting the penny back. Having the chance to make good on her promise. Starting the long and painful process of moving forward. But even though she was maintaining her "this is not a date" stance, a little part of Bree felt the tiny dance of butterflies that a girl usually feels before meeting a guy for a first date. She hated that she felt that way, but she couldn't entirely squash it, even as she pictured Joseph's dad jeans or the aggravating way he'd forced her to meet him on Valentine's Day when all she wanted was the simple, wordless exchange of a coin.

"Hello, again," Joseph said, walking across the square with his mask in one hand. He looked as nervous as Bree felt. "Thanks for coming."

"You didn't give me much choice." Bree realized as she said it that she sounded rude. To soften her words, she smiled. "But I haven't gotten much chance to explore the city yet, so I'm looking forward to that. Anyway, here I am." She tried a small laugh, feeling like everything about her at the moment was completely forced. She needed to relax. "We might freeze to death today, but at least we're out and about."

Joseph looked at the ground and scratched the back of his neck. "Right," he said. "And this is weird, but after all this, I actually still don't know your name."

"Bree Wineland-Jones." She extended a hand to shake his.

"Joseph Mancini," Joe said, taking her hand and holding it for a few extra seconds. Bree looked into his eyes during this extended handshake; they were actually very nice eyes. He *was* good looking, but not intimidatingly so, which was nice. Handsome without the whiff of self-absorption that extremely attractive people sometimes have to them.

He reminded Bree of the boy she'd loved ardently in her tenth grade Geometry class—Derek. Derek Chambers had been good looking in a clean, approachable way, and his eyes had twinkled whenever they talked about congruence and volume during study dates in the school library. So this would be easy: every time she looked at Joe, she'd make her brain think of Derek Chambers. She'd create that positive connection in her mind and thereby force herself to relax a little. Bree exhaled, pleased with this plan.

Joe finally let go of her gloved hand. "Shall we check in?"

They made their way over to a woman in a black coat, black leggings, and a black baseball cap with a heavy scarf wound around her neck. She wore a vest over her coat that read CASANOVA TOUR in red letters. Bree hung back as Joseph spoke to her briefly. The woman pulled a phone from her crossbody purse and double-checked some information. While she waited, Bree considered what they could talk about and how long she'd need to wait before demanding that he hand over her penny.

"She says we're going to start in about five minutes," Joseph said, walking back to Bree with his hands in his pockets. Today he'd chosen a denim Jacket in a slightly different wash than his jeans, and he'd paired the look with red running shoes.

"Those shoes are really...red," Bree said, cringing at the sound of her own words. Instead of waiting for a response to such an inane comment, she forged ahead. "So what do you do, Joseph?"

"You can call me Joe if you want," he said, hands still in his pockets. "And I'm a software engineer. I work for a company based in Australia, but I had the opportunity to work anywhere I wanted, so I chose Venice."

Bree felt herself relaxing. This was good. She could work with this line of chitchat. "Why Venice?"

Joe gave a little shrug. "I just thought it sounded like a cool place and I was tired of cars and traffic and everything else being the way I'd always known it to be. I wanted something different."

"Well, Venice is different than any place I've ever been," Bree agreed. "So the people we saw you eating with—coworkers? Friends?"

"You mean when you fell out of the gondola?" Joe laughed loudly and then caught himself. "Sorry. That was very charming—like something out of an American movie about two women vacationing and ending up in all kinds of hijinks."

His Australian accent was thick and if Bree was being honest, she actually really liked it. It was disarming.

"Yes, exactly." Bree rolled her eyes good-naturedly. "When I went for a swim in a canal with a stupid piece of paper that ended up being totally useless, were you eating with your new Italian buddies?"

"They were guys from my company who decided to come to Italy for a conference. And what was on the paper anyway?"

It was Bree's turn to hide an involuntary smile. "I'm kind of embarrassed to admit it now, but it was a note for you."

"For me?" Joe relaxed and pulled his hands from his pockets.

Bree tucked her hair behind both ears as she looked around the square, watching the comings and goings around them. "I'd been searching for you madly ever since my penny landed on your head, and I had this idea that when I saw you, I'd hold up a note telling you to bring it to the Hotel Chiara, but then—well, you saw what happened."

"And after, you remembered that technology existed and you decided to tweet about it instead?" Joe laughed and folded his arms across his chest, rocking back on his heels.

"Well, my friend Lucy was actually the one who thought of it. She runs a travel agency in Florida, and she tweeted from the travel agency account. Which you saw, so." Bree laughed nervously. "Yeah, I guess it worked."

"Hey, I'm glad it did. And what a way to meet someone, right?" Joe watched her face. "I mean, your penny lands on my head, and we end up connecting on Twitter after a madcap chase through Venice. What a story to tell our grandkids someday, huh?"

The tour guide was approaching them just as he said this, and Bree felt her stomach go into a free fall. The mild case of nerves she'd felt over this whole scenario quickly turned into a full-blown panic. She looked at Joe's friendly face and realized that he was no more related to easygoing, sweet-as-a-golden-retriever Derek Chambers than a pit bull was related to a butterfly. Suddenly Joe appeared to her as a salivating predator, and his presence felt like it was meant to upend her carefully constructed state of zen.

"Oh," Bree said, taking a step back as she shook her head. "I can't do this."

"Hey," Joe said, reaching out to put a hand on her shoulder. His face collapsed into a worried frown. "I was totally joking—I'm sorry. Bad joke. Didn't mean that." As he apologized, Bree knew that her imagination was getting the better of her: there was nothing about Joe that was in any way predatory. This forced date was annoying, but he wouldn't hurt her and in her heart she knew that.

But Bree still felt as if she'd been knocked sideways and she was left trying to catch her breath. *Grandchildren...a future...with someone other than Kenny.* It was something she never let herself think about, even though she knew Kenny wouldn't want her to shut down and live a solitary life for the next sixty years. Her head pounded along with the rush of blood in her veins.

"Yeah," she said, shaking her head. "I still can't." Her voice sounded scratchy and low in her ears, and she stared at his red shoes. "Could I possibly just get the penny? I'm so sorry. I know you're trying to, like," she flapped her hands helplessly as she talked, trying to find the right words, "do some cute thing here, I'm just not up for it."

Joe scratched the back of his neck again as the tour guide stood before them with an expectant look on her face.

"I'm Isabella," the tour guide said, her smile faltering as she looked back and forth between Joe and Bree and realized that the vibe was slightly off-kilter. "Are we ready to tour Casanova's favorite parts of Venice?" she asked hopefully.

Bree looked at Joe. "The penny," she said again, her voice hoarse.

"I don't have it," he finally admitted, looking at her with wide eyes. "It's not with me."

Bree put one hand over her eyes and willed herself not to start crying, but the words she wanted to say got caught in her throat like a fly in a spider's web. Instead of calmly telling him to just drop the penny off at her hotel, she shook her head and gave him a long, imploring look.

"I'm so sorry," Joe said. "I really thought this would be a fun way to see the city, and—"

"Forget it," Bree said, unable to hold back her tears of frustration any longer. "Just forget it."

Without giving Joe or Isabella the tour guide another look, she turned and walked quickly through St. Mark's Square, not even seeing the colorful masks and costumes through her hot tears.

13

FEBRUARY 14
VENICE, ITALY

B ree had shown up at the hotel and immediately gone back to the room, where she paced and muttered to herself as she waited for Carmen and Lucy to return from a trip to Doge's Palace. When Carmen finally got back to the room around four o'clock, she'd found Bree sitting on the edge of the bed, chewing on her thumb and looking angry.

"What do you mean *he didn't have it*?" Carmen's frown deepened as she looked at Bree. She did not handle situations well where people didn't act as expected, and Bree could see her ramping up and gaining steam as she began to understand the situation. "He lost it?"

"He didn't say whether he lost it, he just said he didn't have it. But that was after he said that we'd be telling our grandkids someday about how we met."

"Okay," Carmen said, dropping two plastic shopping bags near the mini bar. She pushed her wind-tossed curls back from her face with both hands as she thought for a second, eyes focused on a spot on the wall. "So that wasn't maybe the *best* thing for him to say, but Bree, he didn't even know your *name* until today. It's not like he knows your whole life history and was looking for ways to freak you out."

"So you think I overreacted?" Bree put both hands to her cheeks, feeling a flush of humiliation. It hadn't occurred to her that she might be the one in the wrong.

Carmen weighed her words for a second. "Maybe a little. I know you were nervous going out with some random guy anyway and that couldn't have helped, but girl, he was just making small-talk. Teasing. Trying to do that awkward first date banter and make a good impression on you."

Bree made a gagging face. "I never *asked* for a date though," she argued. "He kind of forced me."

Carmen nodded, but her face looked grim. "I think it's a miscommunication. He's obviously thinking you're just some cute American girl looking for adventure, and you're actually a cute American girl who is still somewhat...emotionally fragile. But again, he knows none of that." Carmen lifted her shoulders and then let them fall.

Bree released the breath she'd been holding in her chest all afternoon. "I acted like an idiot."

"Come on, girl," Carmen said, pulling her into a hug as she laughed softly. "You only acted like a normal person with emotions."

Bree accepted the hug and then stepped back and folded her arms over her chest. She suddenly felt tired after so many hours of nervous energy coursing through her veins. "So what do I do now?"

Carmen considered this. "Hmmm," she said, sinking onto the couch in their shared sitting area. She crossed her long legs and held out one foot, admiring her own black motorcycle boot with silver buckles as she pondered Bree's question. "Okay," she finally said, dropping her foot. "Let's re-group."

"I'm ready," Bree said. She perched on the edge of the couch next to Carmen, waiting for direction.

Carmen chewed on her bottom lip as she leaned her head back and looked up at the ceiling. "Alright," she said, stretching out the moment as she turned the possibilities over in her head. "So he bought tickets to this tour and you bailed before it even started."

"Ugh." Bree put both hands over her face and let her elbows touch her knees as she bent forward. "Don't remind me. I'm so embarrassed."

"No, come on. It happened and it's whatever now. Doesn't matter."

Bree took a deep breath and sat up straight, squaring her shoulders. "Okay."

"So we sort of blew that," Carmen said kindly. "And now we just need to move on."

Bree sighed and pinched the bridge of her nose.

"I think you need to make the next move, for sure," Carmen went on. "Which is obvious, because he's probably totally freaked out and about to block The Holiday Adventure Club on Twitter and try to forget all about this whole thing."

"Comforting."

"Well, time is of the essence. We need to come up with an idea to fix things."

Bree considered this. "Our only option is to tweet at him."

"Or hire a sky writer. But it's getting dark," Carmen said, looking out the window at the evening sky, "so I think we can rule that one out."

Bree stood up and walked over to the nightstand to grab her phone. "So far we've only messaged him through Lucy's account." She opened Twitter and stared at her personal account, which was mostly unused, given her aversion to anything even remotely social since Kenny died. "Do you think I should use mine?"

"Um, YES." Carmen uncrossed her legs and stood up. "And you need to be charming as hell here, girl. Wait—was he wearing his puffy Australia coat again? Just curious."

"No," Bree said, already distracted as she tried to construct something that would qualify as a mea culpa, a cute overture, and an enticing enough invite to get Joe to give her another chance at getting her penny back. "He was wearing a Canadian tuxedo and a pair of red tennis shoes."

"You mean...denim on denim?" Carmen's face was one of total amusement. "This guy. I swear." She shook her head. "He's as cute as a leading man in a Netflix romcom, but with the fashion sense of a suburban dad."

Bree looked up from her phone. "I know. It's not exactly cutting edge, but I mean, I *was* married to a guy who wore khakis to work and nothing but Adidas on the weekends, so it's not like I'm accustomed to hanging out with dudes who just stepped off an international runway."

"Straight facts there, girl."

"Anyway," Bree said, finishing up her message and handing her phone to Carmen. "What do we think?"

Carmen's eyebrows moved up and down as she read the unsent tweet. She gave a firm nod and passed the phone back. "We like it."

"Okay," Bree said, taking a deep breath and holding it before she posted the message. "Now I'd better get ready and hope for the best."

"I'm running out for Diet Coke again. You get yourself fixed up. Be right back."

LUCY'S PHONE WAS RINGING INCESSANTLY. THE FIRST TIME SHE CHECKED it and realized it was her mother, her thumb had hovered over the screen as she contemplated answering. She'd sent it to voice mail instead of picking up.

The eighth time the phone rang, she was sitting down with the owner of a restaurant on St. Mark's Square about a *prix fixe* menu for the members of the Holiday Adventure Club who wanted to partake of the traditional Sunrise Kiss on the Square the morning after Valentine's Day.

"We can do that, yes," the owner said, scribbling a note on her paper copy of the menu as she squinted at it. "I can make small changes at this point."

"Great," Lucy said. "I really appreciate this."

The bistro was tucked into an ancient looking building that overlooked St. Mark's Square. It had black and white checkered tile floors, marble counters, and antique-looking clocks and fixtures. Though it was currently empty, a small waitstaff in clean white shirts bustled around behind the counters, preparing for the next meal.

"Of course. And would you still like the peach bellinis and crêpes for the pre-dawn breakfast?" the owner asked, sliding her tortoise shell framed glasses off her face and chewing on one end of them as she watched Lucy.

"That would be—" Lucy felt her phone buzz again and slid it from her pocket with a frown. "Excuse me. I'm so sorry."

"No, no. Not a problem." The owner gave her a tight smile—not one of irritation, but that of a busy restaurant owner—and waved her off.

Lucy stood and answered. "Mom?" she said with practiced patience. "I'm kind of busy now. Can I call you back?"

"Lucy," her mother's voice rasped. "Where are you? Are you at home?"

Lucy inhaled sharply to a count of four, held the breath for four counts, and released it for four more. "I'm in Venice," she said.

At some point, Yvette Landish had become the child in their relationship, rendering Lucy the involuntary parent. Yvette's illnesses had been a challenge for both of them, and now that she was in her early sixties, her anxiety, paranoia, and failing memory were causing Lucy even more stress.

"Oh. When can you leave?" Yvette asked eagerly. "I need you to come home."

"I'm not leaving. I'm in Venice, *Italy*, Mom."

"Italy?" Yvette sounded puzzled. "But..."

Lucy did a quick repeat of her breathing exercise, but this time with only two second intervals. *In, hold, release, pause.*

"Remember? I set up a travel program for people who wanted to see the world on all the major holidays? Valentine's Day in Venice?" She made each statement sound like a leading question, hoping that this might jog Yvette's memory. Across the bistro, the restaurant owner was consulting her large, expensive-looking watch as she placed her glasses back onto her face. "Mom, I really need to call you back. I'm in the middle of something."

"But Lucy. I need you," Yvette said, sounding like a frightened child.

Lucy switched gears and softened her tone. "Okay, Mom. I need you to go and turn on the television and watch for about thirty minutes, okay?"

"Okay," Yvette said.

"I'll call you back as soon as I'm done handling this quick meeting. I promise."

With a few more assurances that she'd be back as soon as possible, Lucy ended the call and rushed back to the table. "I'm so sorry about that," she said, putting her phone into her purse and folding her hands together on top of the table. "It's so hard to be away from home, even for a little bit, you know?"

The woman gave her a knowing smile. "Of course. I have children as well," she said, turning her attention back to the menu as she slid it across the table to Lucy with a few small changes. "Will this work for your group? At this price?" She tapped a handwritten figure with her pen, raising one eyebrow as she watched Lucy's face.

"That sounds wonderful," Lucy said. "Again, I really appreciate it."

"Perfect." The owner stood up and offered a hand to Lucy to shake. "Looking forward to seeing all of you after your evening on the town. I'll expect you after five a.m. for breakfast, and the sunrise will be just after seven o'clock."

Lucy shook her hand. "Thank you."

As she walked back out into St. Mark's Square, she considered the fact that the restaurant owner had assumed she was talking to a child on the phone. And it really had become that way at some point: Yvette turning to Lucy for reassurance, comfort, and practical things like arranging home visits by doctors, setting up food delivery, and even registering her disability with the US Postal Service so that they would deliver her mail through a slot in her door rather into a mailbox at the end of a driveway that she refused to even walk down.

There'd been many times that Lucy had wanted to cry with frustration. She'd wanted to shout at her mother: *Why can't you shake this off? You have neighbors your age who meet up to go for walks and play cards, and all you do is sit inside and watch informercials and QVC!* There'd been a point early on when Lucy desperately wanted to call her mother's bluff—to find out once and for all if she was faking this debilitating disease or whether she really was suddenly deathly afraid of crowds and the great outdoors. She'd even considered kidnapping her mother and taking her to Walt Disney World to test out her own theory: once confronted with the Magic Kingdom and all the amusement park snacks a person could want, would Yvette cave and admit that what she was really afraid of was life without the husband who'd left her and the daughter who'd grown up and gone off to medical school?

But in the end, Lucy had done the responsible thing and called doctors and scheduled assessments. After a few appointments, a very kind psychologist had explained to Lucy that most likely, Yvette's condition was a combination of biological factors, life experiences, and real fear, and all that they could really do was to help her and hope that the symptoms would improve with time. They *hadn't* improved, but Lucy was hopeful that whatever hurried trip she used to make from home or work to put out a fire for her mother (Was the Amazon delivery man really standing in her yard staring in the windows? Would she be attacked by overzealous police officers if she mustered up the courage to stand in her own driveway? How come the grocery store had delivered someone else's order and then lied to her and said that no, Mrs. Landish, this really is *your* order?) might be her last trip, and that somehow, magically, Yvette would wake up recovered one day. But then the dementia started around the time Patrick had left her for another woman, and Lucy had felt everything begin to crumble.

Lucy sank onto the bottom step of a church and and watched a group of what appeared to be high schoolers in matching sweatshirts pose in their Carnival masks for photos in various configurations. She fished her phone from her purse and hit her mom's number.

"Lucy?" Yvette answered after one ring.

"Hey, Mom," Lucy said, feeling tired. "What's wrong?"

"I need butter."

Inhale, count of four. Hold, count of four. Exhale count of four. Pause for a count of four.

Maybe this whole life overhaul had been a mistake. Maybe her true place was in Buffalo, close to her mother, and not out gallivanting around, trying to be creative and adventurous. Maybe buying a beach bungalow and trying to put her past in the past was the wrong move entirely. Who was she, after all, to come to Carnival and try to cheerfully guide a group of strangers through a romantic holiday abroad when her only work experience in the past fifteen years involved dismantling cadavers?

"Lucy? I need butter to make mashed potatoes."

Lucy stood up and tucked her free hand into the pocket of her coat. "Mom," she said, raising her chin as she held her phone to her ear. "I'll put in an online order and get your butter delivered today. I'll add a few other things as well, and then I'll check in on you later, okay? I love you."

Without waiting for Yvette to answer, Lucy ended the call. She looked around at the faces of international travelers and people who thought nothing of leaving their regular lives back home and hopping on a plane to see other countries. What made her so different from them? Maybe she *was* the kind of girl to set up a year of adventure for other people. Maybe she *was* the kind of girl to travel the world. Maybe she was even the kind of girl who could help out a new friend.

Before she could overthink it too much, Lucy typed out a quick direct message to @JoeManItaly on Twitter and sent it his way.

14

FEBRUARY 14
VENICE, ITALY

Bree was completely unconvinced about whether or not Joe would respond to her tweet, much less show up at the clock tower. But she'd put her faith in the idea that he'd been acting spontaneous and hopeful with her so far, and so she'd adopted the same attitude.

With encouragement from Carmen, she'd stopped at a little shop and gotten a bottle of red wine, two plastic cups, a corkscrew, and a fresh loaf of bread for them to share. The whole thing felt a bit too much like a date to Bree, but wasn't it, in a way, that very thing? And wasn't she going to have to face that new series of "firsts" at some point anyway?

Her nerves were getting the better of her as she stepped up to the Campanile de San Marco clock tower with a baguette wrapped in paper under one arm and a bottle of wine and the cups in a plastic bag dangling over her other arm.

"Two tickets, please," she said to the girl at the window when it was her turn. "And if I could leave one of the tickets here for a guy named Joe, that would be great." She finished, giving the bored-looking young girl a nervous smile.

"Here you go. Elevator is through that door," the girl said in perfect English, pointing the way for Bree just as she must have done hundreds of times a day for every other visitor.

Bree took her ticket. The weather was not only cold, but the sky was now heavy with what she knew from a lifetime of experience of living in the Pacific Northwest to be sleet or freezing rain—or, at the very least—downright unpleasant precipitation.

With a deep breath, Bree got in line for the elevator and took the lift up to the top of the clock tower. The crowd was thinner than she imagined it might be during the day, and everyone wore heavy coats, thick, knitted scarves, and some combination of hats and gloves. Noses were red, people were hunched together for warmth, and there in front of her was a perfect spot: a bench with a view of the Basilica San Marco and the lagoon beyond. With its rounded domes and tall spires, the Basilica stood proudly against the forbidding sky, its lights shining in the gloom.

Bree sat down on the cold stone bench and set her purchases down next to her. She'd even bought a little red-and-white checkered napkin at the shop, which she spread out next to her. She placed the two cups on the napkin, alongside the bottle of wine and the bread, and as people passed her by, they smiled at her knowingly, probably guessing that she was there on some romantic mission that might end in an engagement or, maybe more excitingly, in a night of unbridled passion. This night would end with neither—of that she was sure.

But it was, in fact, a romantic mission of sorts. Bree could admit that to herself as she uncorked the wine bottle and poured a few inches into a cup for herself. Who cared if she looked sad and alone sipping her vino there, watching the lights of Venice as night fell? She forced herself to sit up straighter and put a smile on her face. There was no reason to look sad—she wasn't sad. If anything, Bree felt empowered. She sipped her wine; it was delicious. Without thinking, she tore off the end of the bread and took a bite, watching as people stopped in front of the open windows and looked out at the city below with arms wrapped lovingly around one another's waists.

Valentine's Day, she thought to herself, taking another bite of bread. She'd never given much thought to how she'd handle each individual holiday without Kenny. Of course she'd considered Christmas and her birthday and their anniversary shortly after he'd passed away, and when those dates had rolled around, she'd dealt with them as every widow must. The first time for each major milestone had been hard—almost impossible, really—but as Valentine's Day hadn't really been their thing, the first one had passed without her giving it too much thought.

But now here she was, in a romantic city halfway around the world, waiting with a bottle of wine to offer a near stranger. The alcohol was soothing her nerves a little, which she desperately needed, and somehow it made the whole idea not seem so frightening. Or wrong. Or improbable. It actually seemed like it could be the necessary next step that she'd been avoiding with too much Netflix and FaceTime with Carmen, and not enough sociability with anyone else.

The people at the top of the clock tower made the rounds and appreciated the view before cycling out, giving way to a new group of people in wool coats and leather shoes, holding hands and nuzzling one another as they whispered sweet nothings in front of a dark sky and twinkling lights. Bree watched them and waited, mindful not to drink her wine too quickly and end up feeling warm and woozy before (if) Joe actually arrived.

When the sun had officially set, Bree exhaled and let her shoulders relax. It was possible that he wouldn't show, and she had to be okay with that. She'd tried to regain the footing she'd lost during their awkward exchange earlier that day, and she'd also tried to take a monumental step toward the rest of her own life here, but even if Joe didn't cooperate, she was still content with the knowledge that she'd tried.

Bree lifted her cup to her lips and slowly took the last sip of wine before she packed everything up to make her way back to the elevator. Around her, people wandered off in pairs and small groups, leaving her there alone for a moment. She stood up and walked to the open window, placing her hands on the wall and looking out as the cold night air touched her face. She closed her eyes and breathed in deeply, glad for a moment that she'd taken this trip, that she'd found the nerve and the fortitude to shake off her safety net and step onto an airplane. No matter how little sightseeing she ended up doing, and whether or not she got her penny back, she'd gone to Venice during Carnival! She'd done that, at least. And she'd worn a mask, made a new friend in Lucy, and eaten a lot of pasta. In the end, nothing about this trip was a loss in her mind, penny or no penny.

Bree took a final long look around at the Basilica and at the people walking on the streets below, then lifted her chin up to the sky, closing her eyes once again. As she did, she felt the first flakes of snow fall gently against her cheeks.

"Bree?"

Her eyes flew open and she spun around to see Joe standing before her, hands in his pockets and a lopsided grin on his face. The rest of the observation deck of the clock tower had nearly emptied of visitors as the wind started to blow snowflakes in through the open windows, and she and Joe were alone.

"It's snowing," Bree said, looking at him with flushed cheeks. "And you came."

Joe looked at the bench that Bree had abandoned, still covered with the checkered napkin, the wine, and the partially eaten bread. The scene almost looked as if it had been staged for a photo. Joe's eyes went back to Bree's face.

"I did come, and it is snowing," he said. "And I have something for you. Well, two things, really."

EARLIER THAT DAY, JOE HAD SEEN BOTH BREE'S TWEET ("I PROBABLY don't belong in a travel club that has to do with adventure, but here I am! Sorry I ruined things this morning @JoeManItaly...would you give me another chance? Seven-thirty tonight at the top of the Campanile de San Marco clock tower. I'll leave a ticket for you at the window."), and he'd also received Lucy's direct message, which he'd opened, read, and responded to right away.

Not long after Lucy had finished coordinating the five a.m. breakfast plans with the restaurant owner and dealing with her mother, she'd met Joe at a little cafe called Dolcevita at his suggestion.

"Can I interest you in a croissant filled with custard and chocolate sauce?" he'd said as soon as he spotted her.

"Um, yes?" Lucy had thrown him a look like the very question itself was complete insanity—did a person really even need to consider that? While Joe ordered for them, she took off her coat and set it over her wicker-backed chair, and then sat down and straightened her sleeves and collar.

"I got you an Americano as well. I hope that works."

"Everything you're saying is ringing my chimes, Joe." Lucy folded her arms on the tabletop and leaned forward with a friendly smile. "Thanks for getting back to me so quickly, by the way."

Joe sat down across from her and leaned back in his chair. "Yeah, of course." He reached for one of the folded cloth napkins on the table and moved it closer to his elbow. "I mean, I've basically spent more time goofing off in Venice in the past few days and less time working than I should, but..." Here, he waved both hands in the air as if to banish the thought. "Eh, who cares? I live alone—I can catch up on emails any time of the day or night."

"That's very sweet of you," Lucy said. "I know my friends and I are basically tweeting at you non-stop," she said, laughing and feeling a tiny bit embarrassed for a second about how high school the whole thing felt at that moment: girl sends message to a boy on behalf of another friend—but then she pushed ahead. "But I need to talk to you about Bree."

The people at the table next to theirs got up noisily, scraping back chairs, putting on coats against the sudden cold snap outside, and saying their jovial goodbyes in Italian. Lucy waited until they'd gone before she went on.

"I shouldn't have joked around this morning," Joe said before she could talk again. A waitress breezed by, set two plates with croissants and two white ceramic mugs of coffee on the table, and vanished again without missing a beat. "I must have said something stupid and set her off. That was my fault." He looked down at his plate and busied himself with stirring a packet of sugar into his coffee.

"Joe," Lucy said, reaching across the table and resting her fingers lightly on the sleeve of his button-up shirt. "It's not that." Joe stopped stirring and looked at Lucy in surprise. She had his full attention. "Bree's husband passed away about a year and a half ago. He had Lou Gehrig's disease, and apparently it was swift and brutal. This is her first trip since he died."

"Oh, God," Joe said. His face blanched. "And I made some joke about us having grandkids someday." As he processed this information, he ran a hand through his dark hair, leaving it a disheveled pile of curls.

"She's over that," Lucy promised him. "But this is where it gets kind of awkward."

Joe had all but forgotten about the coffee and the decadent croissant in front of him. "Okay."

"It's the penny," Lucy said, pressing her lips together before going on. "Her husband wore it in his shoe on their wedding day, and just before he died, he asked her to—"

"Oh, *God*," Joe wailed, thumping the table with both fists. The plates and cups rattled. He didn't even notice when several of the tables around them turned to see what was happening. "No. He wanted her to make a wish with that penny, didn't he?"

Rather than point out to Joe that he'd gotten the attention of nearly half the people in the cafe, Lucy leaned across the table and lowered her own voice. "Yes. And every time she sees you and thinks she's about to get that penny back—"

"I muck it up with my jokes and flirtation." Joe slapped his forehead—actually *slapped* it loudly and comically like a cartoon character—and grimaced. "I should have known I'd be complete rubbish at this stuff," he said in his charming Australian accent. "I was never the type to pull it off, you know?"

Lucy picked up her Americano and held it with the tips of all ten fingers as she blew on the hot coffee. "Pull what off?" She frowned.

Joe's cheeks went slightly pink and he finally glanced around to see who was listening, but almost everyone had returned to their own coffee and pastries. "Dating and flirting and just...*women*."

It was so cute and disarming the way he'd said "*women*" that Lucy nearly laughed out loud, but instead she put the coffee cup to her lips and took a sip to hide her smile.

"Not much of a ladies' man, are you?" she asked, setting the cup back on its saucer.

Joe rolled his eyes. "Not much, no. I went straight to university after high school and dove headfirst into engineering and computer stuff. Of course I've dated—I've even had a serious girlfriend—but I'm just not *good* at it. Do you know what I mean?"

"Actually," Lucy said, picking up a fork and cutting off a small, flaky bite of croissant covered in warm chocolate, "I do. I'm not really much of a Casanova myself. Or rather, a female Casanova," she said, forking the first bite into her mouth and chewing. "Which would be what—a Casanovetta?" She smiled at him, hoping to lighten the mood.

Joe's face instantly relaxed. "Well," he said. "As luck would have it, I was going to take Bree on a tour of Casanova's favorite spots in Venice this morning when I very ham-handedly scared her off. I went ahead and took the tour anyway, and it turns out that Casanova is widely thought of as quite a prolific and accomplished lover, but around here he's rather well known for his gambling habits. In fact, he selected more than one of his female conquests not just for her beauty, but for her financial ability to support his gambling."

"Okay, then I definitely have nothing in common with him!" Lucy said with a laugh, cutting into the thick, custardy center of her croissant. "I'm neither accomplished romantically, nor much of a gambler, so I'll just retract that comparison altogether."

"Fair enough." Joe pushed a lock of hair away from his forehead and reached for his coffee. "But in all seriousness, I really didn't see that

I was going about things the wrong way here. As an objective observer
—unless you already think I'm a massive idiot—" He glanced down at
his croissant before going on. "Do you think a woman who was here
under different circumstances might find me at all charming?"

Lucy watched his face as he raised his eyes hesitantly. There was a
sweet shyness there; just the slightest lack of confidence that honestly
did make him quite charming. That, combined with his slightly
offbeat fashion sense, gave Joe a harmless air and an appeal that was
sort of undeniable.

"Yeah," Lucy said, nodding heartily. "I do. I think that a woman
who wasn't here to start the healing process after losing her husband
might be totally open to the Twitter flirtation. I mean, what a crazy
way to meet someone, right? Her penny falls on your head and you
fall in love. It's a great story."

"It is indeed," Joe said, looking wistful. "It's just too bad it wasn't
the penny of an emotionally available woman that landed on my
head."

Lucy smiled at him sympathetically. "You know, we all have times
where we're more emotionally available than others. It's not a fixed
state." She speared another bite of croissant and dragged it through
the rich custard on her plate before lifting the fork to her lips. "And
what I really wanted to say when I sent you that message is that
maybe Bree isn't ready for a full-blown relationship or even a vacation fling, but she might be ready for a baby step in that direction.
The real question is, are you willing to return that penny to her and
be that guy?"

Joe's eyes had searched her face as he listened. "You mean...could
I be, like, not the guy who wins her heart or anything, but the first
guy to show her that there are still possibilities out there?"

"Exactly."

Joe looked across the cafe to a table in the corner where a young
mother was trying to spoon feed something out of a jar to a happy,
squealing, table-slapping baby in her lap. The corner of Joe's mouth
crooked up in a smile as he watched them. He looked back at Lucy

and gave her a slow nod. "I think I can, and I think tonight I'll have my chance."

"You have two things for me?" Bree asked, standing in the middle of the clock tower that cold Valentine's evening as white flakes of snow floated in and covered the stone floors.

Joe approached her slowly, nodding. "I do. First of all, I have an apology to make. I don't know how to flirt with women and I'm kind of a huge arsehole sometimes." He shrugged, hands still disarmingly tucked into the pockets of his overcoat. "I thought it was fun and spontaneous to try to make you go on a scavenger hunt around Venice for the penny, but that was unfair. I had no idea what meaning it held for you, and I also probably came on too strong."

"No," Bree said, "that wasn't your fault. You were being fun and acting like a totally normal guy trying to meet a woman." She held up both hands so that he'd stop apologizing. "Actually, this would be much easier with a glass of wine. Can I offer you one?"

Joe glanced at the bench. "You brought that for me?"

Bree looked sheepish. "Well. Yes. And then I got into the wine before you showed up. But yeah, I brought it for you." To stop the awkward words from crossing her lips, she walked over and picked up the bottle of wine, pouring a quarter of a cup into each glass and handing one to Joe. He took his hand from his pocket and accepted the drink.

"Thank you. And thanks for saving me the heel of the bread at least."

Bree laughed out loud. "I didn't eat *that* much of it."

"I know," Joe said, taking a sip of the wine. "I was only teasing."

"Can we sit?" Bree scooted over to the end of the bench to make room for Joe on the other side of the napkin, realizing as she did that she must have intentionally set up the wine and bread so that it would act as a barrier between them.

Joe sat on the other end of the bench without comment, drinking his wine as he looked at the falling snow against the night sky and the lights of the city. "Beautiful, isn't it? I hear they weren't expecting this until this morning. It came out of nowhere."

"As many things do," Bree said softly. She sipped her wine.

They sat in amiable silence for a bit, breathing in that cold, crisp smell of snow and appreciating the relative emptiness of the clock tower.

"Do you think they'll remember we're up here and come kick us out soon?" Joe reached for the bread and tore off a hunk.

"I hope not." Bree suddenly felt far more nervous than she'd anticipated feeling. "But Joe," she said. "I want to tell you something. Because I think you're a nice guy."

He groaned. "Oh, the 'nice guy' speech. I'm not entirely unfamiliar with this one," he said, holding up an index finger. "I've heard it a time or two. 'Joe, you're a really snappy dresser and you know a lot of very nerdy things about computers, but this just isn't going to work for me.'"

Bree reached across the wine and bread and took Joe's hand in hers without hesitation. "No," she said. "It's not that. Although you do have a very unique sense of style." They both laughed before Bree went on. "It's about me. Listen, Joe," she said, squeezing his hand and not letting it go. "I was married and my husband died. He had a disease called ALS—"

"I know of it. Lou Gehrig's, right?"

Bree nodded as her eyes filled with tears. "Yes. Kenny was a great guy. In fact," she said, a smile breaking across her face as realization dawned. "He reminds me of you in a lot of ways. Very analytical and into numbers and science—he was a CPA—and frankly, just a nice, organized, reliable, decent man."

Joe exhaled through his nose as he gave a small chuckle. "So some of us *do* get the girl, then. Nice guys, I mean."

Bree nodded and finally let go of his hand so that she could pour more wine into each of their cups. "Yeah, sometimes they do. Anyway, we were happy and thinking ahead to children and grandchildren and a long life together when he got sick. It went fast. I didn't know it would all go that fast…" She shook her head with a faraway look in her eyes. "But it did, and suddenly I was alone with a lot of years ahead of me."

"I'm sorry, Bree. I know that's the right thing to say here and it's never actually enough, but I am sorry."

She gave him a kind smile, her lips pressed together. "Thanks, Joe. It's just such a massive loss, you know? There's no way to fully comprehend it until you're there. And I haven't done any amazing growing or accepting in the past eighteen months, to be perfectly honest. I went back to the bookstore where I've been working for several years and sort of half-heartedly went about my job. Then I came home and watched a lot of Netflix every night and refused to do anything besides talk to my best friend Carmen on the phone."

"Understandable."

"It was, but then I realized it was time to take some very small steps into my future. Carmen told me about this trip with the Holiday Adventure Club, and I remembered the promise I'd made to my husband."

"I think I can guess where this is going," Joe said, looking down into his cup, which was clutched between both hands and resting on his lap.

"I bet you can." Bree cast a sideways glance at him; he was still looking into his wine as if the answers might be floating there.

"The penny was the promise, wasn't it?"

Bree nodded and waited for him to look in her direction. "It almost seems staged, right?"

They locked eyes for a long moment.

"I had no idea when all this started," Joe said. "I never would have used it as a way to pick up a woman. I hope you know that."

"Oh, god! I believe that with my whole heart, Joe," Bree said, putting one hand on her chest for emphasis. "I really do. But he wore it in his shoe on the day we were married, and shortly before he died, he made me promise to take it somewhere good and make a wish with it. So voilà, here we are."

Joe set his wine on the bench between them and reached into the inside breast pocket of his coat. "Which brings me to the second thing I have for you, which is, of course, the penny." He held it out to her in the palm of his hand like an offering. "Please take it with my most sincere apology."

Bree stared at the penny for a long moment as it gleamed under the mellow light. The snow was blowing in sideways through the window now, coating everything in the clock tower with a fine, icy powder.

Finally, Bree reached out and took the penny into her cold fingers. "Thank you," she whispered.

They sat there for a moment as Bree closed her fingers around the coin and shut her eyes tightly, remembering one more time how handsome Kenny had looked as she walked down the aisle toward him on their wedding day. He'd looked both awed and happy as he'd waited for her. She opened her eyes and looked right at Joe.

"For some reason I thought this penny had to be tossed into water so that it could sink to the bottom and hold my wish with it forever like a secret, but I don't think that anymore."

Joe looked at her questioningly, but said nothing.

"Now," Bree went on, standing up and walking over to the window of the clock tower. "Now I think it might bring me more luck if it becomes someone else's wish."

Joe watched her from the bench, afraid to move and break the spell. Her back was to him as she looked out into the snowy night.

"You know how they say finding a penny heads-up is good luck, but if you find it tails-up, you're supposed to flip it over for someone else to find?"

Joe cleared his throat. "I've heard that."

"Well, I kind of think that no matter how you find a penny, it's good luck. So I'm going to toss it from the top of the clock tower and hope it lands at the feet of someone who needs a bit of luck."

The wind howled slightly outside the clock tower, but Bree and Joe were quiet as she contemplated her wish, penny clutched tightly in one hand. Before she let go of it, she turned her head and gave Joe a mischievous grin. "I just hope it doesn't land on the head of some cute guy walking by," she said, winking at him. He laughed and then Bree's face went serious again. "Here I go," she said lightly, holding her hand out through the window.

After about ten seconds of silent thought—really one hushed wish, prayer, and dream all braided together inside of her heart—Bree opened her hand and let the penny fall.

There, she thought. *I did it. I really did it.* She held onto the ledge of the window for a moment, inhaling deeply the smell of late winter before she turned to look at Joe.

"So," she said, swallowing hard against a lump that had formed in her throat. "You've been here with me during a big step in my life, and I have to say thank you for that." Bree dragged the toe of her boot through the white snow on the ground, leaving behind a perfect arc. "And now I have another big favor to ask."

Joe stood up slowly, looking like he wasn't quite sure what to do with his hands. "Sure. Anything."

Bree nodded for a second, gathering the nerve to ask. "I was wondering if you'd be my date for Valentine's Day. Just for tonight," she added hurriedly, holding up a hand. "I'm a slow mover by nature, and I've only got a few more days here, so I'm not thinking about—"

Joe closed the gap between them with just a few steps. He put his hands on both of her shoulders and looked into her eyes. "Just for tonight," he said lightly. "I'd love to be your Valentine's date."

A wide grin spread across Bree's face as she realized that she was making huge strides into her own future right there at the top of an ancient clock tower in Venice. To some they might seem like baby steps, but to her they were wild gallops, and that was okay.

Joe turned on his heel so that he was standing next to Bree. He held out his arm for her to take. "Shall we?"

Bree's smile grew as she slipped her hand through the crook of his arm. "We shall."

They both completely forgot about the remnants of her makeshift picnic on the bench as they walked to the elevator, ready to ride it down to the ground and step out into the snow that glittered beneath the warm lights of Venice.

15

FEBRUARY 14

VENICE, ITALY

L ucy sat inside the bar of the hotel once again, this time next to a window that looked out onto the cobblestone streets beyond. A fine layer of snow continued to gather along the outside sill, ringing the window with frost as a fire crackled in the fireplace across the lounge. It was like a scene from a Dickens novel. The bartender had made her a hot toddy, and she sipped it slowly as she added items to the shopping cart on her phone.

A loud laugh pulled her attention away from the groceries she was ordering for her mother and Lucy looked up in time to see Mrs. Severson and Marge making their way past the opening of the bar.

"Hey there, young gal," Marge called out when she spotted Lucy, waving as she paused in the doorway. "Are you waiting for your date to show?"

Lucy smiled at them. "No, I'm just having a little Valentine's drink here," she said, holding up her toddy. "Are you two off to dinner?"

Mrs. Severson led the way across the hushed bar with its low lights and candles flickering on every table. Marge followed, the tap of her bedazzled cane muffled by the dark carpet.

"You can't drink alone," Mrs. Severson said flatly. "That won't do."

"I'm fine, really—" Lucy protested, phone still poised in one hand, grocery cart half-full.

"Nonsense." Marge pulled out a chair without being asked and sank into it, resting her cane against the edge of the dark wood table. "We'll just have one of whatever you're having and then we'll be on our way. Can't let a gorgeous gal like you sit here alone on a holiday that's made for lovers, can we?"

Mrs. Severson stood there for a moment, looking back and forth between Marge and Lucy. "And we're gonna what, Marge—be her dates?" Mrs. Severson cackled. "No offense, Marjorie, but I'm not sure you could keep up with a young filly like this, even if your taste ran in that direction."

"Oh, sit your big hiney down, Diane," Marge said with a frown and a wave of her wrinkled hand. "Let's get a drink in us before we hit the mean streets, huh?"

Lucy sighed. She saved her shopping cart and locked her phone, setting it on the table next to the candle that flickered inside a small, rounded hurricane lamp.

The bartender saw Lucy's signal for two more toddies and he gave her a slight nod. Marge leveled a serious gaze at Lucy and appraised her from the waist up.

"You got a nice set of knockers," Marge said. Lucy snorted and nearly shot hot toddy from her nostrils. "Pretty head of auburn hair." Her eyes skipped across Lucy's face. "Gorgeous smile and nice cheekbones. All in all a damn fine package. So what's the hold up?"

Mrs. Severson said nothing, but listened to this exchange with great curiosity.

Lucy looked back and forth between the women as the waiter showed up with their drinks. "What's the hold up on what?" she asked.

"Men. A girl like you should have them chasing her all through Italy." Marge looked around facetiously, pretending to search the bar and look under the tables. "By all rights, you should have so much sausage on your tail that you need a bodyguard."

"Sweet fancy Moses, Marge," Mrs. Severson said, shaking her

head. "Are you about to tell us about Simple Jim and his gifts between the sheets again?"

Marge cut her friend a look. "*No*," she said firmly. "I'm going to tell this young gal to sow her wild oats while there are men lined up to do the sowing. Particularly on foreign soil. Better lovers outside the old US of A, I hear," she said, lowering her voice conspiratorially and leaning in closer to Lucy.

Mrs. Severson lifted an eyebrow and raised her drink at the same time. "You know, I'm gonna give you that one, Marge. That's fair advice."

Lucy was totally speechless. In just a few minutes, she'd gone from tossing a pound of butter, some laundry detergent, and a few cans of soup into her virtual shopping cart to have it all delivered to her mother's house more than four thousand miles away, to listening to a couple of septuagenarians discuss the merits of international man meat.

"So," Marge said, smacking the table with her palm loudly. Lucy glanced around to see if anyone was close enough to be as disturbed by all this as she was. "The only thing I can guess is that you're giving off negative signals. Are you sending out some kind of 'don't touch me' vibes to the universe, Miss Landish?"

Lucy sat back in the plush chair for a moment and pondered this. A log in the fireplace crackled loudly and a quiet stream of smooth jazz played throughout the bar. Outside, the snow continued to fall.

Was she giving off 'don't touch me' vibes? Maybe. She lifted a shoulder and let it drop.

"I could be," Lucy finally admitted.

"Is there someone back home? Let's talk about the men on your island." Mrs. Severson set her drink down and laced her fingers together, letting her hands rest on her rounded belly.

Lucy gave a nervous laugh. "My island," she said. "Well, if you've ever been to Florida, you know that the average age there skews a little high. So there aren't really that many eligible men in my age range—"

"Nonsense," Mrs. Severson said sternly. Lucy could imagine her as a bus driver in her younger years, putting middle schoolers in their places all day and handing out disciplinary slips to any twelve-year-old who dared to spit gum out the window or to stand in the aisle while the bus was in motion. "You'll never see us again after this trip, so dish the dirt."

"Okay." Lucy took another sip of her drink. "I've got good looking men on either side of my office. One runs a postal store and the other owns a coffee shop."

"Which one is hotter?" Marge looked ready to salivate at the idea of being wedged between two attractive men—even if it was only logistically and for work purposes.

"Well," Lucy squinted, looking off into the distance as she conjured the faces of the two men. "Dev is really sexy," she let herself say aloud for the first time. "He's serious and kind of your typical guy who loves rock music and wears a lot of black denim."

Marge inhaled sharply and fanned herself with one hand. "Love me a man in denim," she said. "Okay, the other one now—go."

"Nick runs the postal store and he's more intellectual." Mrs. Severson's brows knitted together at this like she was ready to hear that he had a great personality but no physical attributes to match. "And he looks like the hot, young English teacher that all the high school girls would have a crush on. Very 'Just let me read you this one paragraph from the Jane Austen book I'm reading,' combined with the playfulness of a boy who throws a frisbee on the beach for his dog to fetch."

"Oh my stars in heaven..." Marge put both hands to her cheeks as she shook her head. "So what are you gonna do?"

Lucy scratched her eyebrow as she chuckled. "Well. It's not like either one of them is holding up a boombox outside my bedroom window or anything."

Marge and Mrs. Severson exchanged confused looks; this pop culture reference was clearly lost on them, though Lucy was sure there was some generational equivalent out there that was similar to John Cusack blasting "In Your Eyes" in *Say Anything*.

"But which one are you going to go for?" Marge pressed on.

"I like them both as friends and neighbors a lot," Lucy said carefully. "And yeah, I'm attracted to both of them too. I FaceTimed Nick the other day and caught him shirtless in bed, so that was a little awkward."

"Awkward my fat bottom," Mrs. Severson said. "That was a step in the right direction! Next thing you know you'll wake up *next* to him when he's shirtless in bed."

Marge snorted. "How about the other one? The bad boy?"

"Dev," Lucy said. "He texted me the other day and asked me to go to a concert with him when I get back."

Mrs. Severson gave a low whistle. "Girl, you've got more men on that island than you can handle. Who cares about Italian studs when you get to go home to *that*?"

"I guess," Lucy said. She went quiet for a moment. "I've also got an ex on the island who cheated on me with my roommate."

"Yuck." Marge made a face. "Forget about him. He's a nobody in your life story. In the end, he won't even make the cut to be on your greatest hits album—I can promise you that."

"You're so right," Lucy said, feeling empowered by their support. "It's just hard when someone lets you down while you're already vulnerable, you know?"

Mrs. Severson leaned forward and tapped her fingernail against the table three times. "People can only make you feel small if you let them, Lucy. So don't let him."

Her words were like a sunrise for Lucy and she sat there for a moment, basking in the light washing over her. "Exactly. I hear you. God, you're completely on the mark with that one." She sipped her hot toddy and watched the flames of the fire at the other end of the bar.

Mrs. Severson drained the last of her drink and pushed back her chair. "Of course I'm right—I'm old. I know things." She stood up and motioned to Marge. "Come on, old woman. Let's leave this girl to her business and go out on the town, alright?"

Marge got to her feet slowly and leaned on her cane. "These

drinks are on you, right? I mean, in exchange for the nuggets of golden wisdom we just laid at your feet?"

"Of course," Lucy said, smiling at the two women as she reached for her purse. "I've got it. Will I see you both at the sunrise breakfast? All the info is on the daily sheet I handed out this morning."

Mrs. Severson made a noise that sounded like a *harrumph*. "Girl, you will just as soon see me out at sunrise for some group kiss as you'll see me swimming down the nearest canal in my birthday suit."

"I'd pay to see that," Marge said, leaning on her cane.

"Oh, come on, you old cow." Mrs. Severson scowled at Marge and motioned for her to get her slow, rambling gait towards the door of the bar started. "And you," she said, turning around to look at Lucy after Marge had hobbled away, "choose a man who makes you feel like the whole universe lives inside of you. You'll never go wrong with someone who makes you hope that infinity is real."

With a final wink and an uncharacteristically affectionate smile, Mrs. Severson turned and followed Marge out of the bar.

16

FEBRUARY 15
VENICE, ITALY

Bree and Joe took in everything Venice had to offer on Valentine's Day, from a nighttime gondola ride in the snow, to a "masks only" party on a side street that was strung with colored holiday lights and filled with people in Carnival masks dancing to a jazz band comprised of musicians bundled up from head to toe in layers of warm clothing.

Sometime after midnight, they ended up in the Peggy Guggenheim Collection, a museum filled with the most important art works of the 20th century. As they wandered the nearly silent rooms, stopping to look at the works of Degas, Monet, and Picasso, Bree looked up at Joe, who stood next to her with both of their coats over his arm as they browsed.

"This is amazing, Joe," she said quietly. "How did you know that the museum was going to be open all night?"

Joe shrugged and smiled at her. "I hear stuff. And I've been living in Venice for a while now, so I'm learning the ropes."

"Well, this is really special. And it seems like not a lot of people got the memo about the special Valentine's hours."

"Better for us." Joe nudged her with an elbow and nodded at a Jackson Pollock. "Think I'll buy that one to hang in my loo."

"Oh?" Bree laughed. "Let's get them to wrap it up now."

"Tell me more about your job," Joe said, stopping and pausing every few feet as they admired the works that were hung on the walls and lit from above with special lighting.

"I work at Powell's, which is a pretty famous bookstore—"

"I've heard of it," Joe said. "Big as a city block, right?"

Bree's face registered her surprise. "You know Powell's?"

"Occasionally they let us out from Down Under and we're allowed to roam the earth freely. Strange, I know." Joe turned his palms to the ceiling and gave her a goofy smile.

"Oh, they do?" Bree rolled her eyes to go along with her playful mocking tone. "I just didn't know you'd been to Portland."

"Only once," Joe said, holding up a finger as they walked through a doorway and ran into a small group of people dressed for an evening out. The women wore sparkly cocktail dresses and heels, and the men were clad in tuxes with their ties undone. Joe took Bree's elbow and steered her around the slightly drunk and giggling group. "I went to Seattle once for work, and a couple of people on the trip decided to drive down to Portland and check it out. See if it's truly as weird as they say."

Bree nodded, feeling somehow comforted by the idea that Joe had been to her hometown. "The motto isn't 'Keep Portland Weird' for nothing," she said.

"So anyhow, what is it you do at this gargantuan bookstore?"

"I'm a book buyer. Which is basically someone who just...buys books." Bree realized as she said it that it sounded violently boring, but she couldn't think of an interesting way to punch it up.

"You make it sound curl-your-toes-and-hang-on-for-dear-life exciting," Joe said wryly, watching her with amusement.

"Oh, it is," Bree joked. "But honestly, it is pretty interesting. I research the best-seller lists and also make decisions on what I think will do well at our various outposts around town, based on previous sales and customer data."

"Okay," Joe said, squinting like he was thinking hard. "Most recent acquisition that you'd recommend to a thirty-something Aussie who loves science fiction and adventure."

"Oooh, let me think." Bree sat down on a bench in front of a giant painting of a skyscraper done from an extreme angle that nearly gave her vertigo just from looking at it. "I really loved *The Ten Thousand Doors of January* by Alix Harrow. A huge seller and very popular."

"I'll add it to my list," Joe said, sitting next to her and laying their coats across the bench. "Do you ever think you'll do anything different?"

"As in a career? Or just a general life path?"

Joe pondered this. "I guess either. Anything."

Bree turned to stare at the skyscraper painting, cocking her head to one side as she did. "Maybe eventually. I think the idea of doing *anything* differently after Kenny died was unfathomable. For me, surviving the initial stages of grief has been all about familiarity. I needed to keep doing the same things everyday, coming home to the same house, and going to the same job. Until now," she said, rubbing her palms against the legs of her black corduroy pants. "Coming to Venice is wayyyyy out of the ordinary for me."

"Well, good on ya, mate." Joe leaned his back against the wall behind their bench and faced the skyscraper painting, staring at it with his head tilted in the same direction as Bree's. "You're clearing hurdles left and right."

Bree smiled to herself, pleased at the recognition. "Hey," she said, turning to Joe. "How do you feel about pizza?"

"How does any man feel about pizza?" Joe shot her a charming, boyish grin.

"Would you want to get some and then wander around a bit more, then try to make it to the sunrise breakfast that Lucy set up?"

Joe stood and held out his hand, ready to pull Bree to her feet. "I'm game for anything. This is our night on the town."

Bree held out a hand and slid it into Joe's much bigger palm. With a gentle tug, he helped her stand. "Yes," she said, taking the coat that he offered her. "This is our night."

I T WAS PROBABLY CRAZY. I N FACT, IT WAS MOST LIKELY THE HOT TODDY and the hilarious conversation with Marge and Mrs. Severson. Or maybe it was just the heady vibe of Valentine's Day in a romantic city. Who knew? But before she could stop herself, Lucy had her phone in her hand and was sending a message.

I know this day is trite and probably not your thing, but even Neil Young sang about a Heart of Gold, so...Happy Valentine's Day from Venice. Looking forward to the concert when I get back.

Lucy read and re-read the message to Dev before hitting send, then immediately wished she could take it back.

Next, she opened another message and wrote: *I don't want you to ruin my imaginings here by telling me the truth, but on this Valentine's Day, I picture you sitting behind your counter, looking out at the blue sky as you flip through a beat-up copy of Romeo & Juliet and force Hemmie to listen to you read aloud your favorite parts. I kinda miss your face—Happy V Day*

Almost instantly, Lucy's phone buzzed with a message. Dev.

Hey, Miss Adventure. Heart of Gold is actually about a dude who is unlucky in love, but I appreciate your wide-ranging musical tastes. I'm also looking forward to seeing Foo Fighters, and of course to talking work stuff with you. You wouldn't guess that a guy who rides a motorcycle loves business as much as I do, but hey—still waters run deep. Happy Manufactured Romance Day.

Lucy smiled to herself as she read Dev's message for the second time. Her phone buzzed again and she backed out of the message to open one from Nick.

It's like you've got a live webcam in my store! Wait—do you? CREEPER! I don't miss your face, but I do miss you coming next door to bully me about my lack of a fax machine. Have a fabulous day of love in the Floating City. xo Nick and Hemmie

XO? Lucy's heart did a little pitter-patter as she stared at the XO before Nick's name. Huh. It felt weird to be throwing bait at two different fish, but she was operating under the advice of both Marge and Mrs. Severson, *and* Bree and Carmen. What was the harm in some mild flirtation? Neither of them were her boyfriend, and she was just being friendly here. It felt good, flirting. Heck, it was *supposed* to feel good—that was why people did it, right?

"YOU MADE IT!" CARMEN SHOUTED, WAVING AT LUCY FROM A TENTED, outdoor wine bar on the canal that was ringed with standing propane heaters blowing warm air on everyone as they huddled together and watched the snow falling on the water. Even after midnight, the streets were still teeming.

Lucy smiled at Carmen and the man to whom she was standing extremely close. She instantly felt like an interloper.

"Lucy, this is Umberto. Umberto, Lucy." Umberto reached a hand out to shake Lucy's, but he could barely tear his eyes from Carmen's beautiful face. Lucy didn't blame him, really.

"We met—what, Umberto?—like an hour ago?" Carmen tucked herself under her new Italian friend's arm and nuzzled in close, resting a gloved hand on his chest like they were posing for a prom photo.

"*Si*. Maybe an hour," Umberto said, looking deep into Carmen's hazel eyes. "But our love will last many more hours."

Lucy's smile held back a laugh. She desperately wanted to chuckle out loud at the cheese factor of Umberto's slicked back hair, his smooth grin, and the fact that he was clearly on the make. But as she glanced at Carmen, she realized that it didn't really matter, because Carmen was giving off the exact same one night stand energy as Umberto. Lucy leaned over to the bar and ordered a glass of merlot, laying a few euros on the counter as the bartender slid her a drink.

"How's our girl?" Lucy asked Carmen, holding up her glass to clink against both Carmen's and Umberto's before she took her first sip.

"She texted a while back," Carmen said, snuggling in even closer to Umberto's muscular upper body, which was wrapped in a heavy wool peacoat with a bright Scotch-plaid scarf around his neck. "Joe made it to the clock tower and she got the penny. I'm assuming you had something to do with the ease of this transaction?" Carmen eyed Lucy over the rim of her wine glass.

"I might have met up with him and explained the situation," Lucy said with a small shrug. "We needed this to go smoothly, so it seemed okay to divulge Bree's real situation to him."

"Oh, totally. I'm in favor of anything that got that damn penny back in her hands so that we could help her relax. No word yet on where she's going to make her wish, but if she's happy, I'm happy. And her message was full of exclamation points and promises to keep me posted on her whereabouts."

"Wait, are they still together?" Lucy felt bad excluding Umberto from the conversation, but she noticed as they talked that his eyes combed the faces and bodies of every other beautiful woman under the tent. Oh well. Not her problem.

"Apparently. She said they had a good talk, were going to explore Venice, and would meet us for the sunrise breakfast. If I make it," Carmen said, one side of her mouth turning up suggestively as she shot Umberto a look.

"Hey, that worked even better than I thought it would," Lucy said, feeling pleased with herself for arranging the meet-up with Joe at the cafe to explain Bree's frame of mind. "Good for them."

They stood there quietly for a moment amongst the other rowdy drinkers. Lucy sipped her wine. It was clear that Umberto was ready to move their party of two up to Carmen's hotel room or at least somewhere that would require less winter clothing between their bodies, and Carmen continued to nuzzle into Umberto, making it obvious that she wouldn't mind a change of scenery herself.

"You know," Lucy said suddenly, setting her half full glass on the bar and clapping her hands together. She could see her own breath puff out in front of her face as she spoke. "I heard about a dessert tasting at a little place up the road, and I think I'll meet up with a couple of the other travelers from our group and go to that."

"Oh, Lucy!" Carmen said, doing a reasonable facsimile of disappointment at the idea that she would now be alone with her Italian catch of the day. Carmen reached out one gloved hand and grasped Lucy's cold fingers. "I think we're going to see what else is on offer in Venice," she said, giving Lucy a sly wink that Umberto didn't see. It was wholly unnecessary, as Lucy was well aware what was on offer in Venice for them that night.

"You two have a wonderful time," Lucy said with a smile, looking up at Umberto's face. "It was really nice to meet you."

"You too," Umberto said. He raised a hand in farewell. "*Arrivederci!*"

Lucy shoved both hands into the pockets of her overcoat and walked out from under the wine tent. Flakes of snow fell all around her, landing on her shoulders and in her hair, but she didn't mind. It felt good to be alive. Let Carmen and Umberto have a wild fling— she'd tried spending the night with a stranger in college and it wasn't her style, but she didn't begrudge anyone else a little fun.

As she strolled over the cobblestones, she watched all the people in masks who were partying in the streets. Snow wasn't going to slow down the festivities one bit, and everywhere she went, Lucy noticed that restaurants and bars had dragged out heaters and put up makeshift tents wherever they could to create more seating space.

St. Mark's Square was just as full of tourists as it might have been during the day, but the snow made sitting on wet concrete sound less than appealing. Instead, Lucy stood in the center of the open square and took it all in. The old-fashioned lampposts reminded her of, funnily enough, Lumière the candelabra from *Beauty and the Beast*. The warm yellow glow from the bulbs bathed everything in a soft light as people danced around in the snow, some masked and costumed, some not, and she watched everything happily as music blared from a set of speakers on the square. With the falling snow, the colorful masks and costumes, and the rippling navy blue water in the distance, Lucy finally felt as if she were a part of something. She wasn't tempted to dance, but she was caught up in the moment, feeling the beauty of the snow and the camaraderie of being in the middle of a group of people experiencing the same thing.

The important thing to her, as she watched masked couples swaying to an R&B song and children laughing and running around, catching snow on their tongues, was that she didn't feel lonely. Not one bit. She wasn't beating herself up for fleeing Buffalo and leaving the things behind that threatened to suffocate her; she wasn't imagining Charlie and Katrina together at the store, laughing and looking at her basket of candy and magazines; she didn't feel left out because she was in Venice with a tour group full of people who'd all paired off or disappeared into self-made clusters. No, she felt *strong*. She'd done it. Her first trip with the Holiday Adventure Club was looking—at least in this moment—to be a raging success.

Lucy put her arms out to her sides and tipped her head to the sky, letting the snow gather on her cheeks, her nose, her lashes. In the middle of the day in any other city, she might have looked crazy as she closed her eyes and began to turn slowly in a circle, swaying just a little as the music changed to "Heart of Glass" by Blondie, but here in Venice, on a dark, snowy Valentine's night, surrounded by people in Carnival masks and outlandish costumes, she felt free. She felt alive. She finally felt like she'd earned the name *Miss Adventure*.

With a huge smile on her face, Lucy opened her mouth and caught a few flakes of snow on her tongue as she danced. Not a wild dance—just a happy little spin there in the middle of an Italian city.

17

FEBRUARY 15
VENICE, ITALY

The snow had stopped in the middle of the night, leaving a thin coat of frosty white that was just starting to sparkle like glitter under the first pink and yellow rays of the morning's winter sun. Inside the cafe, Lucy sat at a table with a couple from Ohio who'd come along on the inaugural Holiday Adventure Club journey, and she laughed as the wife recounted a story about her twin granddaughters helping one another climb up onto the kitchen counter to eat a full jar of peanut butter between the two of them.

"Lucy!" Bree rushed through the door, breathless. Joe was right behind her.

"Hey!" Lucy stood up. "Excuse me for just a second," she said to the couple from Ohio.

Bree's cheeks and nose were bright pink, and she was smiling from ear to ear. "What a night," she said breathlessly. "I'm exhausted, but I think we saw pretty much everything in this entire city."

Joe was smiling tiredly behind her, hands in his pockets. He had the beginnings of dark circles smudged under each eye. "I'll second that. Bree dragged me around and made me take pictures of everything we saw."

With a laugh, Bree glanced at him over her shoulder and Lucy noticed something different right away: her new friend looked happy. Relaxed. Like a weight had been lifted from her that she had grown so accustomed to carrying that she'd stopped noticing it.

"I'll get us a table for a quick breakfast," Joe said, squeezing Bree's elbow and making his way through the crowded cafe to find an empty table for two right by the front window.

"Well?" Lucy asked, lowering her voice. She was dying to know how the evening had gone.

Bree's eyes danced as she stepped closer to Lucy. "I did it," she said. "I went out with Joe and we had a nice time and the sky didn't fall."

"Good for you!" Lucy pulled Bree into a quick impromptu hug. "And the penny?"

In an instant, a small shadow passed over Bree's face, but almost before it became noticeable, it was gone again. "Got it. Made my wish. Said my goodbyes." Her eyes shone for just a moment with unshed tears. "I think Kenny would be proud."

Lucy barely knew Bree, but even *she* felt proud. "I bet he would," she agreed, feeling her own eyes prickle just a bit with sympathetic happy tears.

"I mean," Bree went on, throwing a quick look in Joe's direction as he carefully carried two cups of coffee on saucers to their table. "It's not like I went on a *date-date*, right? It was just a night out with a friend, but it broke the seal. I survived."

"Definitely," Lucy said kindly, knowing it was what Bree needed to hear. "And now you'd better get some coffee in you quick, because the sun is coming up and people are starting to gather in the square for the sunrise kiss." She nodded at the window and they both watched as people milled about, leaning into one another tiredly after either being up all night or rising early for this snowy kiss at dawn.

It was a nice idea, a group kiss at sunrise, Lucy thought. She sank into a chair as the members of the Holiday Adventure Club trailed out the front door alongside the other early morning coffee drinkers and stragglers. As the sun lifted slowly, peeking over the horizon, people paired off and watched the sky light up as they held hands or stood with their arms around one another.

Finally, someone thought to do a countdown, which—by the sound of it—was conducted in several languages all at once, and when they hit one (and also, *uno, un, ichi,* and *ein*), everyone leaned in to the person closest to them for a kiss. Some were pecks on the cheek, others basically long hugs, and a few engaged in the kind of passionate kisses under the Italian sunrise that looked as if they should be printed in black-and-white and sold on postcards.

Lucy watched it all with a smile as she sipped her coffee. One of the waiters—a young, dark-haired, handsome boy about fifteen years Lucy's junior—was wiping a table nearby.

"Miss?" he said, pausing. "No kiss for you?"

Lucy's cheeks went bright pink and she put a hand to her neck. "Oh! No, I'm in Italy alone. Well, not *alone* alone, but I don't have anyone to kiss."

He set his rag on the table, wiped both hands on the front of his black apron, and nodded at her with determination. "May I?" he asked.

Lucy blinked rapidly. She was exhausted from wandering all night and a bit overwhelmed at the sight of hundreds of strangers embracing outside. Of course she wanted to be a part of it. *Of course* she did. She held out a hand and he took it gently, waiting as she got to her feet.

"I'm Luca," he said, standing before her nervously like a boy picking up his high school date and trying to decide how and if to touch her in front of her parents. Luca looked around the cafe, but the few people still inside weren't even paying attention.

"I'm Lucy," Lucy said. "Ha. Luca and Lucy. That's cute."

He gave a small, polite laugh. "*Buon giorno,*" Luca said, resting his hands lightly on either side of Lucy's waist. "*Sei bella.*"

Lucy put her hands on his shoulders and tried to feel natural as she stood there in an embrace with a complete stranger—and a much younger one, at that. She frowned slightly.

"I said, 'You're beautiful.'"

Lucy's mouth formed the word "Oh," but no sound came out as Luca took a step closer and put his lips to hers.

She closed her eyes and felt the sun pouring through the huge windows as it touched the side of her neck and her cheek. For a moment, Lucy couldn't tell if the warmth she felt was from the sun or from Luca kissing her, but as soon as she settled into the sensation, he pulled away politely. It was a tame, sweet kiss that lasted no more than five or six seconds, but the idea that a young man had seen her and wanted to kiss her, that he had called her beautiful after a night spent roaming the cold, snowy streets of Venice, left Lucy grinning like an idiot.

"Thank you," she said, although it felt a little weird to thank someone for a kiss.

Instead of replying, Luca looked directly into her eyes and nodded once, then picked up his rag and continued to wipe down tables, this time with a half-smile on his full, young lips.

As the crowd started to trickle back into the cafe, Bree rushed up to Lucy and pulled her arm so that they were standing close together. "Girl, *what* was that?" Bree hissed in her ear. "Did I see you making out with a boy young enough to be your..." Bree tried to assess Luca without looking obvious. "I'm gonna be kind here—young enough to be your nephew?"

Lucy shrugged. "Yeah. I guess the sunrise kiss thing got to us, and we were swept away by passion there for a second."

Bree gave her a playful shove as they sat down at a table together.

"Can I get anything else for you ladies?" Joseph offered as he joined them, setting his coat over the back of a chair. Lucy had seen Joe and Bree standing together outside, watching the sun rise in the sky. As the crowd had counted down, they'd eyed one another shyly, but before Luca had come and distracted Lucy, she'd definitely seen Joe bend down and give Bree one totally chaste, sweet kiss before she'd pulled back and put her fingertips to her lips.

In the grand scheme of things, these little kisses might not have been much for either Lucy or Bree, or they might have been completely momentous. Lucy had been reminded by a complete stranger (a younger one! She couldn't forget *that* significant detail!) that she was alive and beautiful and worth the spontaneous romance of a kiss at sunrise in a foreign country, and Bree had climbed her first mountain without Kenny and planted her flag victoriously.

As Joe went to the counter to order a few pastries for them to share, the women reached across the table and clasped one another's hands. They shared a smile of triumph just as the sun cleared the top of the buildings outside, its bright rays warming the cold February morning and bathing the entire cafe in golden light.

18

FEBRUARY 21
AMELIA ISLAND, FL

"Hey, buddy!" A guy in 501s so worn in that they looked like tissue paper stopped and leaned over to slap Dev's hand. Dev and Lucy were sitting in the middle of a huge grassy area on a blanket, waiting for the concert to start as they drank cold beers out of a cooler that Dev had brought along.

"Hey, Gus. This is Lucy," Dev said, introducing them. Lucy looked up from her perch on the blanket and smiled at Gus, whose beard was neatly trimmed around a straight, white smile. The men launched into a conversation about the bands that were going to play that night while Lucy took a few pulls on her beer and looked around.

The late February evening was typical Amelia Island: the day's completely blue sky had morphed into a fiery sunset, and the high had only been in the mid-sixties. With darkness approaching, Lucy could feel the chill in the air and she pulled her jean jacket around her torso, glad for the extra layer over her white t-shirt and thin, olive green cargo pants.

"I'll catch you later, man," Gus said, reaching out to slap Dev's hand again and then lifting his fingers casually in the air as a farewell to Lucy. "Nice to meet you," he said, disappearing into the crowd.

"Sorry about that," Dev said. "Gus and I used to work together."

"Not a problem—seriously." Lucy gave him a smile. "This is great. Just being here." She looked up to watch as a few especially persistent stars began to poke holes in the evening sky.

The Foo Fighters had been confirmed to play, as had a few other bands that were slightly outside of Lucy's wheelhouse, but they were all on Dev's list of "must see" shows and Lucy could feel his excitement.

"You're going to hear some great stuff tonight," Dev promised, picking at the label on his beer bottle and tearing off a piece. Lucy watched him; he wasn't prone to nervous fidgeting, and this seemed out of character. "Wilco, Stereophonics, Filter."

Lucy set her bottle on the grass next to the blanket and pulled her knees to her chest, wrapping her arms around them. "I'm looking forward to it."

A not totally awkward but not entirely comfortable silence fell between them as the group of young women on the blanket in front of them passed a vape pen back and forth, blowing their clouds up into the sky to impress one another.

Lucy had gotten back from Venice riding a high after having pulled off the first trip with the Holiday Adventure Club successfully. Without hesitation and in spite of layovers in both Moscow and New York City, Lucy had ignored her jet lag and showed up at her office the morning after landing in Jacksonville, throwing herself into planning for the next trip with total abandon. And with her feet on the island once again and her key poised in the lock of her office's front door, it had hit her that she'd been flirting via text (and Face-Time, if you counted her call to Nick) with both Nick and Dev, and now she'd spend her days sandwiched between them again, trying halfheartedly to ignore the fact that she was somewhat attracted to both men.

"So," Lucy said, reaching for her beer bottle and taking another drink. "Got any great ideas for the Holiday Adventure Club?"

Dev turned his head and looked at her as he leaned forward, resting one elbow on his knee and letting his beer bottle dangle from his hand. He glanced at the stage where a group of sound and light techs were frantically crawling around and testing things.

"Listen," he said, sounding a lot like someone who was trying extremely hard to be nonchalant. "I heard you asked Nick to go to St. Barts with you next month. Is that true?"

Lucy wasn't expecting that. "Uhhh...in a way. I guess. We talked while I was in Venice and somehow it sort of came up that he should come." It sounded like she was avoiding the truth, and Lucy looked away from Dev, glancing at the people on the blankets around them.

"So." Dev smiled, looked like he was about to say something, paused, then started again. "So, what exactly is up with you two. Are you a thing? Am I at a concert with another guy's girl?"

"No," Lucy said quickly. She looked back at Dev and made eye contact. This was the absolute truth; she wasn't Nick's girl by any means. "We're not a thing. We're friends—like you and me." Ugh. That didn't sound quite right either and it definitely made it seem like she was trying to gently friendzone Dev with a soft landing. And was she really "just friends" with either Nick or Dev? Did she *want* to be just friends with either or both of them? Lucy winced and tried to come up with something that reshaped her last statement, but nothing materialized.

Dev nodded and looked at the toe of his boot as he hooked an elbow around his own knee. "Well," he said, casting a glance in Lucy's direction. "I guess we are friends. I just like to know where I stand, you know? It's no secret that Nick and I don't really get each other's vibe, but I don't wish him any ill will. I just don't want to be fighting him for the attention of the same girl."

Lucy's heart started to race. Dev saw himself as fighting Nick for her attention? She tried to casually put her fingertips to the pulse in her neck to check and see whether it was pounding as wildly on the outside as it felt like it was on the inside. It was.

The animosity between Dev and Nick was nothing major, so far as Lucy knew. It was something dumb, like, when they'd all moved into the strip mall and become neighbors, Nick had ordered a coffee at Beans & Sand and then complained that it was a little weak. Oh, and it was *possible* he'd also mentioned that he thought The Beatles were overrated as he paused to look at all of Dev's band posters in the coffee shop. And *maybe* he'd once ranted that unless a man was James Dean, if he rode a motorcycle after the age of thirty, then he just looked like a midlife crisis waiting to happen. Then Dev had slandered J.D. Salinger (one of Nick's favorite authors) and made some crack about being a middle-aged man with a frisbee who picks up teenagers on the beach, and things had gone downhill from there.

So there were a couple of minor things they didn't agree on.

Lucy pulled her thoughts together. "Well," she said, watching the stage intently as the huge colored lights flickered and changed their pattern in a test run by the sound techs. "I can honestly say that I'm currently nobody's girl. I enjoy your company and I enjoy Nick's company, but you're totally different guys."

Dev gave a huff as if to say *Hell yeah, we're different*, but he said nothing.

"I think you're really cool, Dev," Lucy said, more softly this time. "And I was looking forward to hanging out with you the whole time I was in Venice."

Dev looked her way again, this time with a smile. "Hey, I was looking forward to it, too. Thanks for coming." He leaned over and bumped her with his strong, t-shirted shoulder and as he did, Lucy caught the scent of clean soap mixed with something rich and musky, like cloves and burning wood and vanilla. He smelled so good that she had to stop herself from leaning into him for another sniff.

Since he'd brought up Nick and St. Barts, it seemed like a good idea to steer the conversation away from the upcoming trip and back to more neutral ground. "Hey, quick question," Lucy tipped her head at the stage. "Best Foo Fighters song?"

"I'd say the acoustic version of 'Everlong,' but I'm also a huge fan of 'Walking After You,'" Dev said, letting go of his knee and stretching his long legs out in front of him. He crossed his boots over one another and leaned back on his hands, facing the stage.

"Okay, best Stereophonics song?"

"It's completely underrated, but I love 'Maybe'—how about you?"

The corner of Dev's mouth turned up; he obviously knew that she wasn't as into these bands as he was.

"Uhhhh," Lucy said, pretending to consider the question. "I'm open to all of them," she finally said, stretching her legs out in front of her just as Dev had done. She put the palms of her hands together and wedged her hands between her knees. "But truth be told, I'm more of a 70s music girl. I grew up on Fleetwood Mac and Todd Rundgren. Stevie Wonder, Billy Joel, The Eagles—stuff like that."

Dev nodded and put his hands together as if in prayer, bowing his head. "Much respect. Good stuff," he said. "That's the beautiful thing about music, in my humble opinion: there's something for everyone, and your taste never stops growing and changing. Maybe you'll leave here tonight a huge Wilco fan."

Lucy laughed. "Exactly! You never know."

"I'm pretty stoked about this." A smile like Lucy had never seen spread across Dev's normally placid face and for a second he looked like a little kid on Christmas morning. She could even see the outline of the cute, curly-haired boy he must have been, with his polished teak skin and rich, brown eyes.

Lucy took another sip of her beer as she continued to watch his face in profile. *Cute,* she thought. *Cute, smart, interesting, slightly unknowable, a little mysterious. Definitely trouble.* She gave a slight shake of her head and looked back at the stage as the lights dimmed and the first band made their way out from backstage, taking their places without fanfare.

The lights went low for about twenty seconds and a hush fell over the crowd and spread across the grass. Dev leaned back, eyes focused on the stage as Lucy looked his way one more time. Then, right on cue, the lights blasted the stage and Filter launched into the opening notes of "Take a Picture."

The crowd went wild and Lucy raised her bottle in the air, shouting excitedly along with everyone else.

19

FEBRUARY 22

AMELIA ISLAND, FL

"It's nice to see that you didn't turn so cosmopolitan and international that you don't have time for us little people anymore." Nick heaved a box full of packing tape onto the counter of The Carrier Pigeon. He pulled a box cutter from the back pocket of his jeans and sliced it open.

"Oh lord—as if," Lucy said, reaching down to scratch Hemingway's head as he lay sprawled in front of the bank of P.O. boxes along one wall. If anyone wanted to come in and fit their key into the lock of the box they were renting, they had to bypass this half-alert sentry. Lucy smiled at the thought of Hemingway guarding anything; he was easily the sweetest, most laid-back dog on the planet.

"Seriously. I thought you'd come home holding one pinky in the air while you drank your coffee."

"I didn't go to England," Lucy said with a laugh, giving Hemingway one last scratch before she stood up.

"Or wearing a beret and smoking cloves."

"That would be Paris—didn't go there either."

"Well, you know what I mean." Nick glanced up from unpacking the rolls of tape and gave her a half smile. "We missed you around here, though."

Lucy watched him stacking the tape on the counter and walked over to help. "Here, hand me some rolls. I'll make another stack." She held out her hands and waited as Nick loaded her up with tape. "And it's nice to be missed. It's also nice to be home."

The front door of The Carrier Pigeon was wide open and a light winter breeze was blowing through the shop. Dev and Lucy had stayed for the whole concert and while she'd limited herself to one bottle of beer before switching to Diet Coke, she still felt exhausted from being out until two in the morning. With the back of one hand, she brushed a strand of hair off her forehead and shoved a tower of tape rolls aside so that she could keep stacking.

Nick took the empty cardboard box and cut the bottom with his blade, folding it and tossing it into a pile of flattened recycling.

"So how was the show last night?" he asked with his back to her.

Lucy swallowed. She'd purposely *not* mentioned to him that she was going to the concert with Dev, but their proximity throughout the day combined with the fact that everyone on the island seemed to know each other's business meant that it was almost inevitable that Nick would hear about it one way or another.

"Good," she said, trying to keep a casual lilt in her voice. It had been a good show, after all, and there was no reason for her to pretend otherwise. "I have to admit I didn't know many songs by anyone but the Foo Fighters, but it was still a really excellent show."

Nick nodded and rested his hands on his narrow hips. "Glad to hear it." He gave her a smile that felt slightly forced. "Really glad to hear it."

Lucy looked around the shop. "You need help unloading anything else around here?"

"Shouldn't you be back at the office planning for St. Barts?" Nick cocked his head as he watched her. "This is a pretty quick turnaround time for you, from Valentine's to St. Patty's Day."

But Lucy didn't want to leave. Sure, she should be back at the Holiday Adventure Club headquarters, answering emails from the travelers who'd be joining her in the French West Indies in just a few weeks, making plans for excursions and activities on the famed island, and double-checking travel plans and flights and whatnot, but somehow standing there with Nick on a sunny morning in the middle of the postal store, listening to John Mayer's latest album as they stepped around Hemingway and worked together on little projects was way more fun.

"I guess I should," Lucy finally acquiesced, looking longingly at the way the sun was warming Hemingway's black fur. "But if you can afford even a part-time assistant, just give me a shout and I'll come back and work with you anytime."

Nick laughed. "I'm sure I'd do far more business with you behind the counter than me."

"Don't count on it," Lucy said, walking towards the open door.

"Hey," Nick called out, catching her just as she crossed the threshold. "I was thinking a bit more about taking a vacation from all of this." He spread his hands wide and turned from side to side theatrically, as if looking out over his mighty kingdom. "And I'm considering asking my sister to come down and watch the shop for a week so I can join your travel group. Do you have room for one more?"

Lucy could see the trepidation on his face—the way he'd almost not brought it up for fear of even a minor rejection. She knew that her answer here, including how long she hesitated before saying yes or no, was going to change their friendship in ways that couldn't be undone.

And so she didn't hesitate at all: "Absolutely," she said with a smile. "If you're serious, we leave March 15th and get back on the 23rd."

Nick digested this. He actually looked a little shocked, as if he'd been expecting her to brush him off. "Yeah," he said, running a hand through his already mussed hair. "Yeah, definitely. I'm serious. Let me check with Krista and see if she's really up for coming down here and running the show."

Lucy stood in the doorway a second longer, smiling at him as the sun that covered Hemingway's fur ran its rays across her arms and legs and warmed her from head to toe.

"Okay, just let me know." She patted the doorframe twice and walked out onto the sidewalk. Maybe she'd stop in at Beans & Sand for a cup of coffee before sitting down to her email.

A GROUP CHAT BETWEEN LUCY, CARMEN, AND BREE WAS KEEPING HER from a phone call with the hotel in St. Barts, but she kept laughing and smiling as the women shot messages back and forth from across the country.

Girlllll, Carmen said. *I'm so proud of you! You went to the concert with Hottie #1!*

I have LOTS of questions, Bree said. Instantly, Lucy imagined Bree at a desk in a tall building in downtown Portland, the February rain pouring down the windowpanes as she sipped a cup of coffee from a nearby Starbucks and tried to keep her feet warm with heavy wool socks under her boots. *Did you kiss him? Is it a thing? Does Hottie #2 know?*

How did we distinguish who was Hottie #1 and Hottie #2? Lucy typed back. She chewed on the lid of a pen as she waited to see who would respond first.

Um, obviously whoever takes you out first becomes Hottie #1, Carmen shot back.

Okay, then yes, Hottie #2 (Nick) knows I went to the concert with Hottie #1 (Dev) last night, and this morning when I was next door in his shop talking, he brought up the fact that we'd sort of talked about him going to St. Barts with me in March.

OMGOMGOMGOMGOMG, came Carmen's response.

Well this escalated quickly. Hang on—phone call at my desk. I guess they're paying me to work while I'm here. BRB. Bree's message came through and then she went quiet for a few minutes.

I'm also getting paid to work while I'm here, but this is more interesting, Carmen said. *So riddle me this, Batgirl: what is #1 gonna say when #2 goes on a sexy island vacation with you?*

Uggghhhhh, Lucy typed back. *Idk! He brought it up last night because he'd already heard about it, but you two know the scoop—neither of them is my boyfriend! The concert was the first time I'd ever done anything with Dev AT ALL besides drink his coffee!*

Didn't #2 buy you a snow globe before your trip or something sweet like that? I feel like you told us that...which technically would make him #1... damn. Do we have to rename them?

DON'T CONFUSE ME EVEN MORE!!! Lucy added emojis of a wailing face and a face with streaming tears.

I'm back, Bree said. *What did I miss? Oh, yikes. I'm all caught up. Here's my verdict before my ten o'clock meeting with my boss: kiss them both and see which one gives you butterflies. Report back. Gotta run! xxx*

Said the girl who had a panic attack when some perfectly nice Australian guy joked about them having grandkids together someday, Carmen added.

I heard that. You two behave.

Lucy laughed out loud at Bree's final words, then slipped her phone into the drawer of her desk so she could spend a few hours focusing on the tasks at hand. She was exactly three weeks from getting on an airplane to a far-flung island, and she had more to do than flirt with Nick, take in concerts with Dev, and chit-chat with her new girlfriends on the West Coast. (Although it did give her a warm rush of happiness to realize that she *had* new girlfriends to talk to about anything at all.)

With a sigh, she lifted the phone on her desk to listen to her voice mails and get started on her afternoon To Do list.

20

MARCH 3

AMELIA ISLAND, FL

"So this is really happening?" Nick ran a hand through his hair as he looked at Lucy in the early evening light. They were both closing up shop about an hour before sunset, standing in the parking lot with their keys in hand as they leaned against their respective cars. Lucy could feel the scrape of her chipped and rusting paint as it caught on her gauzy skirt, but she ignored it. There'd be time (and hopefully money) later on to get a fresh coat of yellow paint on her Bug.

"I think it's really happening," Lucy nodded, folding her arms across her chest and looking out at the cars rushing by on the street in front of the strip mall.

"I haven't left this shop in five years. I don't even think I've taken a sick day," Nick said, looking impressed with himself. "Not to mention leaving Hemmie."

"Oh, he'll be fine," Lucy said, waving a hand through the air as she crossed her feet at the ankles and relaxed against the door of her car. "Your sister sounds totally capable."

"She is," he assured her. "Krista knows more about business than I do."

"Then you're gonna have to let go and just have fun." Lucy gave him a smile as the breeze blew her loose hair around. A strand caught in her eyelashes and she reached up to brush it away.

She was still unsure how it'd happened, but in less than two weeks, she and Nick were headed to St. Barts and it seemed that Dev had accepted this fact and was now using it to keep things slightly chilly between them. In fact, just that morning he'd poured her coffee wordlessly and turned to the next customer, letting one of his baristas ring her up instead of doing it himself with their usual back-and-forth banter.

"I'm pretty stoked," Nick admitted, pushing off from the side of his old Volvo and turning around to unlock it. Lucy glanced at the backseat and smiled with amusement when she realized the whole bench seat was piled high with books.

"Just in case you get bored at work?" She nodded at the traveling library.

Nick threw her a look over his shoulder. "I can never decide what to read next, so I just bring every book I own."

"Seriously?" She laughed.

Nick's smile widened. "No, ding-dong, I'm not an eccentric millionaire. I was going to drop those off at the used bookshop, but I got busy and forgot."

"You were going to drop them off and get more, weren't you?"

"Busted." Nick grinned as he tossed his messenger bag onto the front passenger seat and turned to her one more time. "Anyway, I'm excited. I hope I don't slow you down on this trip. In fact, I promise I won't. I know you have travelers to attend to, and I really want to just...be helpful if you need me, but also lay on the beach—"

"With a book," Lucy interrupted.

"With *several* books—and get some time to relax and forget about running a business. That dictates like 90 percent of my life, you know? Wake up, work, handle everything until bedtime. Wake up, repeat everyday until death."

"Be careful who you joke about death with," Lucy teased. "I can horrify you with as many interesting factoids about corpses as you could possibly want to hear."

Nick ran a hand through his hair. "You know, I always forget entirely that you had a whole other life before this one."

Lucy looked out at the street again. "As did we all, right? I'm sure you weren't a postal store owner from the second you graduated from college. You've had a life."

"You're right," Nick said. "Funny how as adults we don't start our friendships and relationships with the whole info dump of our past. We work our way into it."

"Don't want to scare each other off entirely within minutes, right?" They exchanged a smile. "But truthfully, heard and understood about getting away from it all for a while," Lucy said, holding up a hand in the air like a silent *amen*. "There is no rest for the wicked —or the business owners of the world."

"Truer words were never spoken." Nick pulled his car keys from the pocket of his cargo shorts. "Okay, I'll see you tomorrow. I'm sure Hemmie is waiting eagerly by the door for dinner and a walk." Nick lifted a hand in farewell and then slid behind the wheel.

As he pulled out of the lot and onto the main street, Lucy watched him, still leaning against the side of her car. It was a gorgeous evening, with a muted pastel sky. A walk on the beach wouldn't hurt her at all, but she'd skipped lunch and her stomach was roaring like a lion. As she drove out onto the main street, Lucy contemplated her options: Cook? Takeout? Leftovers? She was considering a quick stop at the store for a roasted chicken and a fresh baguette when her phone rang.

It was her mother.

After a brief internal tug-of-war over whether or not to answer (there was never any question, really), Lucy picked up.

"Hi, Mom."

"Honey, I don't feel good. My heart is racing. I think someone is trying to break in."

Lucy squinted at the road ahead of her as she held the phone to her ear. She knew she should probably pull over and talk to her mother properly, but this conversation wasn't a new one.

"Okay, tell me what's going on," Lucy said calmly, swinging her car into the lot of the grocery store and parking between two giant SUVs.

"The guys who were mowing the lawn next door were at my window. I could see them looking in," she said in a rush, sounding frightened.

Lucy pulled her keys from the ignition and grabbed her purse. She really wanted to get home with her groceries and kick off her shoes, so she held the phone to her ear and locked the door as she talked. "Were they actually peering in your window, Mom, or just walking by as they did their job?"

Yvette sighed deeply. "You know, I'm not sure," she admitted. "It looked like they were staring in my windows and I almost called the police."

"You're not allowed to call the police anymore for things like that, Mom," Lucy said firmly. This had become an issue with her mother and the local police, and at one point, Lucy had been on a first name basis with the cops who'd responded numerous times to Yvette's impassioned phone calls begging for unnecessary assistance.

"I know," Lucy's mom said, sounding annoyed. "But how is a private citizen expected to protect themselves if not by calling the police?"

Lucy walked through the sliding doors and into the frigid AC of the store. She lifted a basket from a stack and walked right for the deli where the whole roasted chickens would be boxed up and waiting under a heat lamp.

"Okay, but we have to have reasonable expectations, Mom. They can't use their manpower to respond to Yvette Landish every time a landscaper passes too close to your window while you watch daytime TV."

There was an icy pause between the women as Lucy stood before a basket of fresh-baked baguettes and listened to the muzak version of David Bowie's "Modern Love." A woman with a baby in a cart paused near Lucy and the baby reached out and brushed its chubby fingers against the paper that was wrapped around the bread.

"I only call when I don't feel safe, Lucy," her mother finally said.

She was clearly offended that her only child wasn't taking the situation seriously enough.

The woman with the baby moved on and Lucy's eyes dropped to the floor. She suddenly felt exhausted. "I know, Mom. I'm sorry. But I need to weigh these situations and try to help you from a distance. I'm doing my best," she said softly.

"You could move home," Yvette suggested, sounding hopeful.

Lucy laughed, but it was a quiet chuckle; this wasn't a new conversation either. "Mom, Amelia Island is home to me now. I live here. I have a house and a business."

"And now you're leaving the country—what, every other week?"

Lucy nodded, though she knew her mother couldn't see her. "Several times this year, yes. And it's something I need to do."

"Who do you need to prove yourself to? That guy who left you for the rude girl with the back tattoo?"

This time Lucy's laugh bubbled out audibly.

"It's just a little vine with roses along her lower back," Lucy said, wondering instantly why she would even bother to defend Katrina's tramp stamp. "But you're right, she *was* rude."

"Still is, I'm sure." Yvette sniffed.

"Quite possibly." Lucy lifted a baguette and stuck it in her basket before moving on. "But no. I need to prove it to myself that I can take this journey. Plus I wanted to do something big with my business. Something more than book airline tickets for businesses and set up mid-priced hotel banquet rooms in Ohio for their corporate meetings."

Yvette was silent for a moment. "Take me with you," she said.

"Mom." Lucy stopped walking and moved to the side quickly so as not to be steamrolled by an older man hunched over his shopping cart. "That's impossible."

"There are pills for my condition, Lucy. I can take medication." It sounded like she was begging.

Lucy set her basket on the ground and put her fingers to her forehead, still holding the phone with the other hand. "I don't think that's a great idea," she said, trying to be as gentle as possible. She didn't have the heart to remind her mother that she was already taking a fistful of pills each morning and evening and that they didn't seem to be doing much besides holding her steady for the time being.

"I'll go wherever you're going, Lucy, and I'll behave. I promise." Her mother sounded like a child trying to negotiate a later bedtime or a second helping of dessert. "Just take me."

"Mom." Lucy's eyes filled with tears. Hearing her mother plead made her feel like a child. She felt like someone who couldn't fix the things that were broken even though she desperately wanted to.

"Fine," Yvette said, hearing the unsaid words. "Then what do I do if something happens while you're gone?"

"Aunt Sharon is there, and I've found caregivers—"

"No," Yvette said loudly. "I do not want to be put in an adult care facility. No."

"That might be something we need to talk about eventually." She tried to sound soothing and not patronizing. "I can't ask Aunt Sharon to manage everything, and having someone professional come and stay with you twenty-four hours a day might be more expensive than living in a residential home. But we're not there yet."

Yvette remained silent.

"Look, there isn't any other option right now, but I'm doing the very best that I can."

"You're going to lock me in a home and forget about me. That's how it happens, Lucy."

Lucy rubbed her forehead and looked up as a young grocery store clerk in a green vest paused to re-stock a shelf of canned corn. She gave him a half-smile.

"I need to finish my grocery shopping, Mom. I'll call you later, okay?" Lucy disentangled herself from her mother as gently as possible and ended the call.

Leaving on these trips for a year would be a monumental task and she'd known that going into it. But it was also imperative to her that she did this. She *had* to. And not to prove anything to anyone but herself. The predicament of how to keep tabs on her mother from another country was one she'd anticipated, but that didn't mean the actual heartbreak of loving and caring for an aging parent was lessened by the excitement of adventure abroad. It had been a weight on her shoulders for several years, and as her mother aged and progressed, that weight seemed to double and triple exponentially—sometimes faster than she could keep up.

Lucy checked out absentmindedly, paying with a credit card and getting into her car as the sun tickled the underside of the palm fronds. It was nearly dark by the time she pulled into the driveway of her little bungalow and collected her plastic shopping bags and her purse.

It wasn't until she was in her kitchen, setting everything on the counter that she realized she'd completely forgotten to buy chicken.

Hey, Lucy texted Nick that night as she lay in bed. The lamp was on next to her. She pushed her glasses up her nose and kept typing. *Are we really doing this?*

I'm afraid we are, came the quick reply. *Second thoughts?*

About going to a far-flung tropical island when we already live on one?

The three dots that meant Nick was typing seemed to hang in the text box forever. Finally, his reply: *No, that you agreed to let me tag along.*

Lucy chewed on her bottom lip, thumbs poised over her phone, a book open on her chest. *Not a single second thought on my end*, she said. *You?*

No way. I'm packed and ready.

No one can handle a fax machine like you, Mr. Epperson. How will the senior citizens of Amelia Island get by without you to send off their notarized documents and whatnot? Lucy smiled at her own joke.

The same way mid-sized companies will plan their own corporate retreats in your absence.

Lucy smiled to herself. *Ahh, but I can still do those things from afar. I just log in from the balcony of my hotel room overlooking the water and book Acme, Inc. on a trip to Poughkeepsie for their annual shareholders meeting. Problem solved!*

Hmm. You're right. Oh well...I'll let my sister handle it all—she was alive in 1990, so I'm sure she can fax like a beast.

Let's get some rest, Lucy typed. *There are adventures ahead and we need our beauty sleep.*

There were no dots for a minute as Lucy stared at her phone. Finally, she picked up the open book on her chest and stuck a bookmark between the pages, setting it on her nightstand along with her glasses. The snow globe of Venice that Nick had given her was next to her lamp, and she studied it for a moment, marveling at the fact that just a few weeks earlier she'd been wandering the Venetian streets and canals, drinking wine, meeting new friends, and watching people dressed for Carnival swarming all around her.

Just before she was ready to turn off the lamp and roll over in her bed, a final text buzzed her phone.

Get some sleep, Miss Landish. We've got a big trip ahead of us and The Holiday Adventure Club ain't seen nothin' yet...

Lucy set her phone down and rolled onto her side, pulling the blankets around her snugly. She fell asleep with the moonlight on her face.

READY FOR THE NEXT BOOK IN THE HOLIDAY ADVENTURE CLUB SERIES?

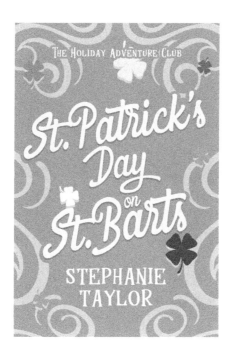

Join The Holiday Adventure Club as they take a trip to the French West Indies for St. Paddy's Day. Buy from your favorite bookstore here!

ALSO BY STEPHANIE TAYLOR

Stephanie also writes a long-running romantic comedy series set on a fictional key off the coast of Florida. Christmas Key is a magical place that's decorated for the holidays all year round, and you'll instantly fall in love with the island and its locals.

To see a complete list of the Christmas Key series along with all of Stephanie's other books, please visit:

Stephanie Taylor's Books

To hear about any new releases, sign up here and you'll be the first to know!

ABOUT THE AUTHOR

Stephanie Taylor is a high-school teacher who loves sushi, "The Golden Girls," Depeche Mode, orchids, and coffee. She is the author of the *Christmas Key* books, a romantic comedy series about a fictional island off the coast of Florida, as well as *The Holiday Adventure Club* series.

https://redbirdsandrabbits.com
redbirdsandrabbits@gmail.com

Made in the USA
Las Vegas, NV
10 April 2022

47163210R00095